THE DAY THE CEILING
FELL DOWN

The Day the Ceiling Fell Down, Jenifer Wayne's
second novel for children, was first published in 1961,
and contains all the characteristic elements of what
was soon to become a classic Wayne story. The humour
and ordinariness of family life lie at the centre of her
writing, and in this novel, and its sequel *The Night the
Rain Came In*, we share in the upheavals, disasters,
triumphs and confusions that make up the lives of
Louisa, Japhet and Rose Brown, their harassed parents,
and Oats the dog.

Unexpected developments in the plot and vividly
realistic dialogue are also features of Jenifer Wayne's
writing, while her skill at sketching in her characters
with a few swift but sure strokes has been likened by
one critic to that of Stella Gibbons.

Jenifer Wayne's many other novels for children
include *Someone in the Attic* and *The Smoke in Albert's
Garden*, and she is also very well known for six stories
for younger children about a little boy called Sprout.

Born in London in 1917, and educated at Somerville
College, Oxford, Jenifer Wayne worked as a writer and
producer for the Features Department of BBC Radio
from 1941–1948, when she married the journalist C. H.
Rolph. She died in 1982.

THE DAY THE CEILING FELL DOWN

Jenifer Wayne

THE BODLEY HEAD
LONDON

British Library Cataloguing
in Publication Data
Wayne, Jenifer
The day the ceiling fell down.—(Bodley bookshelf)
I. Title
823'.914[J]   PZ7
ISBN 0-370-30799-2

Copyright © Jenifer Wayne 1961
Printed and bound in Finland for
The Bodley Head Ltd
30 Bedford Square, London WCIB 3RP
by Werner Söderström Oy

First published by William Heinemann Ltd 1961
This edition first published by The Bodley Head Ltd 1986

Chapter One

'I don't think we have any tea made,' said Louisa, knowing perfectly well they hadn't, but trying to sound polite.

But the tramp just stood there at the door; the evening sun dazzled, shining off the empty glass beer bottle in his hand.

'I'll go and ask,' she said. '– But we've only just come home.'

They had been at the lake all day; the wet bathing things were still dumped in a soggy tangle on the back grass ('lawn' to visitors). Rose and Japhet, of course, had gone straight in to look at television. (By the way, his being called Japhet was to do with a grandfather; it was nobody's fault.) They *would*, thought Louisa, who was fourteen and sometimes felt older. And all this mess to clear up. The kitchen table was littered with the remains of two picnics: part of a cut loaf, a bag of banana skins, some squashed tomatoes, half a bottle of now luke-warm orange juice, and a plastic box of oily butter. It had been the hottest day of the year. They were all exhausted and rather cross after so much bathing and sunbathing; their mother had gone up to change.

'Could you come?' called Louisa.

'No!'

'There's someone at the door.'

'Tell them to wait.'

Louisa went half-way up the stairs. 'Please come, it's a tramp and I don't know what to say.'

'Oh really, this is the last straw!'

Louisa stared. Her mother stood on the landing with an ash-white face and grey hair. For a moment Louisa thought she must have been taken ill – then she saw the dress. Once red, it was now white on the shoulders, shading down to pale pink; and the sunbeams that slanted through an open bedroom door were packed with spinning dust.

'Mother – whatever's happened?'

'Go and look,' said their mother grimly, and came downstairs. '– It's *your* room,' she added over her shoulder, '– and I'm not making tea now, if that's what he thinks!'

But the tramp only stood looking blank. He was a tall, youngish man with an obstinate red face.

'I can give you some water,' said Louisa's mother.

'I don't want water.'

'I'm sorry, but we haven't any tea,' – and then, as he scowled at her disbelievingly – 'We only drink coffee.'

Now why say a silly thing like that? She could never refuse anybody outright: it was a standing joke with the family. Their father still teased her about the time when she had had the piano tuned twice in one week because 'this second poor man was a new one and he looked so sad.'

'Coffee'll do,' said the tramp, and handed her the bottle.

So when Rose came into the kitchen to ask if they

6

could have the other programme, she found her mother standing like a pillar of dust by the gas stove, angrily boiling milk.

'Who's that for?' asked Rose. '*I* don't want hot milk.'

Rose was seven, and still felt bitter about the time when they had made her drink it in hospital, after having her tonsils out. 'It makes my throat go all funny –'

'Ssh! You can give him one of those buns we left – there, in that greaseproof bag.'

'Who? Where?'

'Mother! It's an *awful* mess!' Louisa appeared in the kitchen with as long a face as a roundish person can have.

'What is?' said Rose, bewildered. She liked to get things straight, one at a time.

'Not *that* bag, silly, that's eggshells –' Louisa, at fourteen, was apt to be impatient with this slowness. Rose was still carefully folding over the edges of the the wrong bag, with her straight fair hair falling forward in two points, when Louisa had screwed the top of the tramp's bottle, wiped it, put a bath bun in with an old cheese sandwich, given them to him, and shut the back door.

'Well, you couldn't go like that,' she said to her mother. Louisa was convinced that while some mothers seemed to manage all right, hers needed looking after.

'I don't think he'd have noticed.'

'Who? Noticed what? *What's* a mess?' Rose was getting worried; at any minute now she would start crying, as she easily did when she was tired, and people wouldn't explain.

'Well, just look at mother's dress: look at her hair! Don't you know what's happened?'

Rose gazed up with surprise. Her mother was there, that was all that mattered to her – though she took a great interest in her own appearance, and spent whole minutes at the bathroom mirror.

'You've got bits,' she said. 'You look all crumby.'

'My dear child,' said Louisa, 'go and look at my bedroom!'

'I say, I tried to turn it over but the picture's gone all funny.' Japhet came in, wearing nothing but his bathing trunks, the second pair; his hair stuck up in stiff tufts, dried in the sun; his face had gone pink over the freckles; and he was chewing.

'Could you come and see? Please hurry, I'm missing Gunbusters!'

'You and your Gunbusters – you'd better come and help *us*,' said Louisa. 'And take away that disgusting bubble-gum!'

'Why, what's the matter?'

'My ceiling's fallen down, that's all. Nearly my whole ceiling! It must have happened while we were out.'

'Gosh, let's see!' And Japhet rushed up the stairs three at a time, followed by Rose, who looked pleased and frightened.

'Gosh!' said Japhet again. 'Was it like this after the bombs?' He was ten, and liked to hear about war.

'But who did it?' said Rose.

'Nobody did it, silly, what d'you think?'

'A giant might of,' said Rose.

'Might *have*,' Louisa corrected her.

'But what shall we do? Will Louisa have to sleep here?'

'Clear it up, I suppose,' said their mother.

'I can't possibly sleep here' – Louisa started to cough – 'I should choke.'

It was a very small room, with sloping walls and a single cottage window; at the moment it was like a little box of rubble and hot white fog.

'I say, it looks as if some more might come down,' said Japhet hopefully, and he prodded the ceiling where a jagged edge of plaster hung from the papery-looking laths. A crumble, a crack, a crash – and then Rose's most ear-splitting yell.

'Now look what you've done!' Louisa gasped through the mess and din.

'Rosie, what is it? What happened?' Their mother staggered over the crunching plaster and put her arms round Rose, whose shrieks at last turned into the words 'My head! My head!'

'Let me see.' She pulled Rose's hands away from her face, which was brown under streaks of tears and dust.

'You do look funny!' said Japhet, and Rose yelled louder then ever, but this time with rage.

'You know she doesn't like being laughed at,' said Louisa. Rose did fuss too much, but there was no need to make her worse. 'How would *you* like to have a ceiling on your head?'

'It was only a bit. Of course she would have to stand just where –'

'Japhet, go and get a broom,' interrupted their mother. 'You can start clearing up.'

'But I wanted to look at telly,' he began, and then saw the blood on Rose's hair as her mother carted her off to the bathroom. 'Anyway, how was I to know? I was only testing it.'

'Well, you know now,' said Louisa – and then, because he really looked guilty and upset – 'Come on, we'll need a dustbin for all this plaster. Whoever would have thought there'd be so much from one small ceiling?'

'And so heavy,' said Japhet, lifting up a piece about the size of a dinner plate. 'I say – look here!'

'What?'

'There's some paper sticking on to it with writing – look! Gosh, this might be valuable: suppose we found the clue to a hidden treasure –'

'Don't be batty, this isn't television. Let's have a look.'

'Here's some more!' said Japhet excitedly. '– And look, there's a whole lot in that corner, all rolled up!' He dived into a heap of plaster and pulled out a small bundle. Louisa peered over his shoulder, then sighed and stood up.

'My dear boy, bits of old newspaper.' She tried to sound off-hand, to cover up her own disappointment – though of course she was much too old to believe in hidden treasure; she had almost given up reading stories about it.

'Probably what the workmen wrapped their sandwiches in: look, *Daily Mail. Now* will you come and help?'

'There might be something else up there, though,' said Japhet wistfully looking up at the straw-and-plastery laths and the dark cracks between.

'Yes, mice,' said Louisa. 'And don't you go touching it again. Come on.' And she marched off to get brushes and pans.

Japhet followed – but not before he had taken the pieces of newspaper and stuffed them carefully into his own sock drawer. You never knew, there might be something written on them in invisible ink . . . words marked to make a code . . . some lost formula. . . . Girls, thought Japhet, really are dim. If it had been his room, he wouldn't have been in any particular hurry to clear it up. You could make roads and mountains for the cars to race round, with all that plaster – and caves for plastic Indians. He would have left it like that for a week at least.

However, by the time their mother had washed Rose and given her some juice and a cut-up apple in bed, Louisa and Japhet had moved a lot of the plaster from the floor on to themselves, and some of it into the dust-bin. Japhet kept glancing up into the roof.

'I'd love to see what's up there. *How* old is this house supposed to be?'

'Three hundred years in front, about a hundred at the back,' said Louisa promptly. She had made sure of this when they moved in, a year ago.

'Well this is the front. Who was king, three hundred years ago?'

'Heavens, I don't know,' said their mother wearily. 'It's too hot to think.'

'Charles the First, I suppose,' said Louisa, who happened to have been doing him at school.

'D'you think he slept here?' said Japhet.

'No – why on earth should he?'

'Well, kings and those people did sleep in places. I mean, he had to sleep *some*where,' Japhet persisted. 'I say, if I did find a mouse, could I keep it?'

'More to the point,' said Louisa, 'would be where am *I* to sleep tonight?'

'With Rose,' their mother announced out of a cloud of dust. 'We'd better get out the camp bed.'

'Oh can't *I* sleep on the camp bed?' said Japhet. 'It's not fair, Louisa always——'

'Nothing's fair,' Louisa interrupted decisively. Their father had often told them this, to stop arguments.

'Shall I take these sheets off?' she asked – and then '*Oh!*' She stood aghast.

'What's the matter now?'

'My costume! Oh Mother, look at my costume!'

Underneath a pile of rubble on the white bedspread lay Louisa's clothes for the school play. Velvet jacket, white blouse, pyjama trousers dyed brown (the stripes didn't show much).

'– And my hat! Look at my hat!'

'The hat's the worst,' said Japhet. He put it on and started to do his imitation of Donald Duck.

'Oh shut up!' Louisa snatched the hat from him and looked at it with a very red face. 'It's all squashed, and the feather's broken! And I spent ages painting that feather red!'

'Perhaps you can find another one,' said their mother.

'Not like that. And it has to be big, Miss Bleakie said so, or it won't show up.'

'You can have one out of my Indian set if you like,' said Japhet generously. Louisa, generally so calm, was nearly in tears; and anyway the Indian set was quite old.

'And we can brush the other things, don't worry, dear.'

'It's all very well, I have to be on the stage the whole time, and it's the dress rehearsal on Monday.'

'Well, we've got tomorrow,' said their mother wearily, 'Now will you help me carry this dustbin down?'

By the time they had fairly cleared the room, they were grey from head to foot, and the gas had been left on under the empty milk saucepan.

'Whoever wanted hot milk anyway?' asked their father when he came home to a black wave of smell. He had been playing cricket, away, for the village, and his shirt was sticking to his back. He poured himself out a huge glass of cider while they told him about the ceiling and the tramp.

'Now we'll be getting them by the dozen,' he said. 'Didn't you know they have a secret sign they put outside the house?'

'What sort of sign?'

'To tell their fellow-tramps this is a good place to stop. A "cup of tea here" sign.'

'I suppose you mean "mugs here",' said their mother, smiling wanly.

'It was coffee,' Louisa pointed out.

'– But I didn't give him any sugar,' their mother added, looking brighter.

'Perhaps they've got a sign for "bring your own sugar",' suggested Japhet.

'Go to bed,' said his father. 'And don't forget tomorrow's Sunday. No shouting before eight. *Or* electric trains.'

'But do you really think we shall get a lot of tramps now? We could make a sort of hotel for them in the chicken-house –'

'Go to *bed*!'

'A hotel for tramps – really!' Louisa smiled when he had gone; she rather enjoyed having a quiet laugh with her parents about 'the children'.

'Well, why not?' Japhet had come back for his torch, which was at last discovered in a casserole on the mantelpiece. 'It might be jolly good; you might get one who was really a millionaire only he'd lost his memory, and then when he found it he'd give us some of his money and –'

'Here,' said their mother, 'take an apple. And that doesn't mean you don't have to clean your teeth.'

'All right,' said Japhet. 'But all the same, you never know.'

Perhaps this was the truest thing he had said that day. Certainly none of them could foresee that on Sunday something would happen which would make them forget even fallen ceilings and old newspapers.

Chapter Two

The morning started off quite normally, except that Rose had a lump on her head.

'It's as big as an egg,' said their father, gently feeling it.

'Hm. A smallish egg.' Louisa liked to be accurate. Besides, Rose was rather too proud of these things. Japhet was right, it *would* be Rose who was standing just where the plaster fell. She was what Louisa had heard called 'accident-prone'. If there was a wasp around, it stung Rose; it there was a nail to sit on, Rose sat on it; if a log fell off the woodpile, it would be sure to fall on Rose. And a toffee from the bag kept in the medicine cupboard was never enough; Rose had a passion for First Aid. So her hands, knees, heels and elbows were always either covered with bits of frayed grey-pink Elastoplast, or rimmed with black marks where the last piece had been. Her record was three plasters, two bandages and a black eyeshade for a stye.

'Can I go and show my lump to Mr and Mrs Gillings?' she asked at breakfast.

'Don't swank,' said Japhet. 'Always wanting to be petted.'

'I'm *not*!' And she scratched him with a sharp piece of toast. Then Japhet dabbed her with an eggy spoon, and they had to be separated.

'All right, you can go with Louisa and get the Sunday papers,' their mother said. 'And perhaps Japhet will take Oats out for a walk, then I can get on.'

Oats was the dog; the name was his colour. They had always been promised a dog when they came to live in the country, though their father now said that if Oats was anything to go by, the safest place for dogs was town. They had already had two phone calls from farmers complaining about him, and once the local gipsy had come to the back door insisting that he had had her best cockerel. This was not true; on that particular day, Oats had a perfect alibi. He must have a double, they argued, though none of them could really believe this. There couldn't be two dogs with spaniel ears, no tail, greyhound legs and a face like a sooty old man's. Rose once wanted to cut his whiskers with nail-scissors, but Japhet said that would be cruel because they were part of his way of feeling.

'Feeling what?' asked Rose.

'Things round corners,' said Japhet.

'But what things?'

'Oh, how do I know, I'm not a dog!'

'Does a dog know it's a dog?'

'What else would it think it was?' said Japhet.

Still, he was a lovely dog, and they were sure he could go as fast as a camel, which someone had told Japhet was the fastest animal in the world. Unfortunately they had to try not to let him go anywhere at all without someone close behind him; he was too fond of sheep. Their father had made a 'puller-tugger' – a clothes-line with a sliding ring and a long chain attached, on which any normal dog, he said, should be satisfied to have the run of the garden. But Oats didn't think much of this at all, and would sit looking reproachfully at the house until someone came out and unhooked him.

But on this particular Sunday morning, Japhet was not pleased at the idea of a walk, so he put Oats on the tugger and hoped no-one would notice when he went up to his room to have another look at those papers. His torch battery had given out last night; also, he had gone to sleep.

Louisa and Rose sat in Mr and Mrs Gillings's front room; they had paid for the papers which Mr Gillings always got for them on Sundays, but Mrs Gillings had asked them in for biscuits, so of course they went. Louisa hoped Rose wouldn't say they had only just had breakfast: she knew the Gillingses had been getting up at six for forty years, rain or shine, because they had told her so – and she was rather ashamed of the way her family muddled about on Sunday mornings, having breakfast at any old time in torn jeans or bits of frog-mens' outfits. Besides, she always wanted a biscuit.

But Rose was too full of her lump to say anything tactless. Mrs Gillings was very sympathetic, and called Mr Gillings in from his bean-sticks to see it, which made Rose wriggle back into the big armchair, beaming with approval. Of course they wanted to know how it had happened; here Louisa took over, judging that Rose had had as much limelight as was good for her.

'I expect it was shrinkage,' Mr Gillings said. 'The plaster shrinking in all this 'eat.'

'Of course, there weren't such a thing as a bathroom when we were there,' Mrs Gillings added. 'I dare say he had that put.'

'Ah,' said Mr Gillings, ' 'E 'ad a lot put, soon as 'e got us out.'

'Who did?' asked Rose.

'Mr Glover. He were the owner as took over and had the house knocked into one. Of course, that little room you speak of, that were the Captain's.'

'Ah, that'd be 'is 'alf,' nodded Mr Gillings, sucking his pipe. 'Poor old Captain, we never did know what became of 'im.'

'That's funny,' said Louisa, 'we found an old board with "Captain's Cot" written on it – Japhet's got it in front of the chicken-house now.'

'Ah, that'd be 'is old sign, what 'e 'ad outside 'is front door. Course, that door's blocked up now. Mr Glover properly pulled the old place about, when 'e got clear of us.'

'I dare say it's made very nice, mind,' said Mrs Gillings politely. 'What with the electric in, and the water and all.'

'We 'ad to draw every drop from the well in our time. Beautiful water it was, though, like crystal. None of this disinfectant they put in it nowadays.'

'Were you very sorry to leave?' Louisa asked.

'No, I can't say that,' Mr Gillings admitted. 'Mean to say, 'e did find us this place, which being a bungalow means less running about. Course, with the Captain it were different. 'E'd been born there, see, so it was only natural 'e should want to 'ang on. They do say 'e **threatened Mr Glover out of a window with a rabbit-gun once, though 'e were a peaceable chap enough, given 'is rights.'**

18

'But what happened – did Mr Glover just turn him out?'

'That's right. Served two or three notices on 'im to quit, but the Captain only tore 'em up. "You'll not get me out of 'ere alive", 'e'd say – but 'e were properly alive all right the night they come to shift 'im. Ranting and raving, you could 'ear it right over the common.'

'But what became of him, where did he go?'

'That we never knew. It was an evening in May, and there was 'is furniture stuck out all over the path, some of it thrown on the grass in front, and the Captain sat there on 'is old rocking-chair bawling and carrying on something alarming. Oh, 'e didn't 'alf create.'

'I remember it,' said Mrs Gillings, 'because the laburnum was out, and it did seem so unnatural. There he sat, rocking away, with the yellow bits falling on his hair, and such language! Well, we tried to reason with him, but Sam pulled me off; "such words is not fit for you to hear", he said. I suppose he picked them up at sea.'

'But what happened?' Louisa persisted. 'He couldn't just sit there all night.'

'It were a mystery,' said Mr Gillings. 'Next morning, Mrs Gillings sent me round to say we'd take 'im in for the time being; "tell 'im to come for breakfast, any rate," she said.'

'I'd got some nice rashers, and the hens had been laying lovely; I put a big brown egg aside special –'

'– But it was no go. 'E'd 'opped it.'

'Gone?'

'Clean off. Seven o'clock I walked across the common, the way you've come this morning. I could still see, 'is things standing there in the sunlight, lovely day it was too. When I got up to 'em, though, they was all wet with dew – 'is bedding and everything, drenched. And no Captain.'

'And we never saw 'im again, that day to this,' Mrs Gillings added with an air of gloomy triumph. 'Poor old chap, I shouldn't wonder if he finished up in a home.'

'But he *had* got a home,' said Louisa indignantly. 'You said he'd been born there.'

'Ah, but it was Mr Glover's by rights. We only paid rent, Mr Glover bought up the two cottages for a song, at a time when we couldn't afford to refuse. We needed the money – so did the Captain, I reckon, seeing his expectations hadn't worked out right.'

'We used to tell 'im, you can't live on expectations, but 'e wouldn't listen. Obstinate as a mule, 'e was; proper old character.'

'D'you mean he expected to get some money?'

'Ah,' said Mrs Gillings, 'that was the shape of it. 'E was always thinking somebody'd leave 'im something in their will. Regular will-mania 'e 'ad. Used to study the papers every day in case there was one of these adverts for a missing heir. You know, these columns where they put for anybody who was a relative of the late so and so to get in touch with the lawyers, and they'll 'ear something to their advantage. But 'e never did.'

'What he kept saying,' said Mrs Gillings, 'was he had some rich uncle out Australia way –'

'New Zealand.'

'– Well, one of them parts. Anyway, he thought it

were about time this uncle passed over; "I can't understand it", he used to say, "he *must* be dead by now". Not that he was a heartless man, not at all, though I used to tell him he shouldn't talk like that. But he said why not, it's only nature; we've all got to die. "What's more," he said, "when I get it, I'll give you £100 for a holiday and £20 on top of that for a new hat and coat". Poor old Captain, he was a good sort really.'

'Was he actually a sea captain?' asked Louisa.

'That's what he called himself, but we never knew. He'd not been to sea for years, though he always wore his navy-blue jumper and his sailor hat, blue with a little black peak.'

'And he used to dig turnips in 'is sea-boots,' added Mr Gillings. '– And 'e carried a compass everywhere. Quite an upstanding man 'e was, well-spoken, too, when 'e wasn't swearing. I often wonder what become of 'im.'

'Have another, dearie,' said Mrs Gillings, and handed Rose the biscuit barrel, yellow china with a Ramsgate crest on the side. Rose chose a custard cream, and wished they had a barrel like that at home.

'We must be going,' said Louisa, 'they'll be wanting the papers.'

'Wait a minute, I wonder what I've got here –' and Mrs Gillings started to rummage about in a sideboard. Rose began to smile, and looked sideways at Louisa, who frowned at her. Mrs Gillings's sideboard was a wonderful thing: in its drawer she always 'found' something, as she put it, for 'any little visitors'. And although Louisa could hardly be called little, she was

21

as pleased as Rose to be given a small bar of chocolate or a pencil with traffic lights on the end or a paper flower that opened out in water. This time there was a lavender-bag for Louisa, a stick of red sealing-wax for Japhet ('I know boys; anything they can put a match to,' smiled Mrs Gillings) and for Rose, a tiny blue plastic yacht out of a cereal packet.

'We saved it for you; you put a spot of detergent on the end, then it's jet-propelled,' Mr Gillings explained.

They walked home across the common. Twice Rose dropped the yacht in the long dry grass, and Louisa had to find it for her. They both got very hot as the sun now blazed straight overhead.

'I'm going to be boiling in that play,' said Louisa. 'Right out there in the middle of the games field, and I have to be on the whole time – and in those clothes. Oh dear, those clothes! Let's look for a feather. Japhet's Indian ones are all mucky, Oats chewed them.'

'Why do you have to be on the whole time?'

'I've told you about a thousand times, I'm the Narrator.'

'I thought you were a woodcutter,' said Rose. 'And not a thousand times.'

'Well, the Woodcutter *is* the Narrator.' Louisa thought Narrator sounded better; more distinguished.

'It's funny for a woodcutter to wear pyjamas,' said Rose, 'with a velvet jacket.'

'*You* don't know what woodcutters wear,' snapped Louisa.

'Would this do?' Rose handed her a tiny fluffy white feather from a bramble bush.

'No,' said Louisa, 'it wouldn't.' Then she was rather sorry for sounding so cross, and picked Rose a handful of wild raspberries; there were quite a lot of them on the common if you knew where to look, and didn't, like Japhet, pick unripe blackberries by mistake. Rose immediately dropped them all into the long grass, which made Louisa cross again, and she was too hot to stop.

'Wait for me!' wailed Rose, scrabbling about. Louisa walked on, very slowly and thoughtfully. Across the road, beyond the cricket pitch, was their house, which had once been the Captain's. There was the laburnum tree where he must have sat; there was the window, out of which, perhaps, he had pointed the gun at Mr Glover. Louisa saw him as a blue-eyed old man with white hair and a brown face. Mr Glover, she imagined, was fat and pale, with a thin mouth and little eyes too close together, and a bowler hat. The more she thought about him, the more she detested Mr Glover. Poor Captain! What became of his furniture, she wondered. More important, what became of *him*? And there had she been, sleeping in his room all this time, while somewhere he was wandering about, turned out of house and home; perhaps eating grey porridge in some horrible lodgings; perhaps even sleeping out, like a tramp. . . . She pulled the tops off the mauve feathery grasses, feeling guilty and sad – until Rose called out, 'I've found a beauty!' In her hand was an enormous, prize pheasant's feather nearly two feet long.

'I just looked,' she said proudly, 'and I found it. Is it just what you wanted?'

'Yes,' said Louisa affectionately, 'it's just what I wanted.'

'Perhaps if I looked again, I could find another hat. Well, the gipsies do throw things away in the bushes.'

'Not hats. Besides, it'd be dirty. I shouldn't think they often wash their hair.'

'Tell me something else to find,' said Rose.

'Hm. Find the Captain,' said Louisa briskly.

'He's not a thing.'

'No, but he's lost.'

'*You* find him, then.'

Louisa stopped, gazing at the house, which looked back at her with open windows, the walls like thick cream in the sun, the blue paint fading in a friendly way. She suddenly thought of that poem beginning:

> 'I remember, I remember
> The house where I was born . . .'

'All right,' she said. 'All right, I will. Well, there can be no harm in *trying*.' She sounded calm and matter-of-fact, but really she felt as if she had just had an electric shock.

'What will you do?' asked Rose as they crossed the road.

'I shall have to think.'

'When will you start?'

'I don't know. Now.'

'Now? D'you mean you'll go and look in the wood?'

'Don't be barmy, how can he have been in the wood all these years? The Gillingses left ages before we came.'

'He wasn't there yesterday,' said Rose thoughtfully,

'because I went to get a stick.'

Louisa didn't answer; she was too full of her new idea.

'– And don't tell anyone!' she called, as Rose rushed in to try out her yacht.

'Not even Japhet?'

'No!' – Anyway, not yet, Louisa added to herself. It might be a wild idea, but it needed planning. Japhet would either laugh, or he'd jump at the wild part and not wait for plans. Then he'd go and do something ridiculous, and let the whole cat out of the bag. Rose, though so small and slow, was much more reliable. She could keep a secret. And this, thought Louisa, might be the best secret I've ever had. She felt like a mixture between missionary and detective; it was a feeling that gave you the shivers, even on a hot Sunday morning.

But when she got into the house, things were in such a state that there was no question of looking for the Captain that day at all.

Chapter Three

First, the breakfast things weren't washed up. And their father was on his hands and knees in the cupboard under the sink. And Japhet was rubbing Oats with a towel already covered with mud.

'Mud?' asked Louisa. 'Mud, on a day like this?'

'The main's burst,' said their father, coming out from among the saucepans with a cobweb on his ear. 'I've managed to turn it off,' he added. 'By the way, is this that old cullender you were looking for? It'd make a good helmet.' And he put it on his head.

'The arrows'd come through the holes,' Japhet objected.

'But what's happened?' said Louisa. It was difficult to make her parents be serious.

'We've no water, that's all,' her mother told her. 'The pipe's burst out there, it's all been coming through into the garden.'

'Oats discovered it,' said Japhet. 'It was just where he was sitting on his tugger. I looked out, and there he was, rolling in mud! You could hear it gurgling up; it's like a swamp out there.'

'I want to see,' said Rose, and ran out.

'But what can we do?' Louisa asked, dismayed. 'We won't be able to wash!'

'*That* doesn't matter,' said Japhet. 'We'll get nice

26

hard skins. They say dirt protects you.'

'Who says? – Anyway, what about drinking?'

'Milk,' said Japhet.

'I drew off a couple of bucketsful, and some in the bath,' their mother said, 'but when that's finished, we'll have to go to the Carters.'

'What, carry it – all that way?' Louisa collapsed on to a kitchen chair; she was hot enough already, and the thought of carrying buckets half a mile and back down the road. . . .

'Besides,' she said, 'the Carters are so terribly posh; they'll be all dressed up for church, and they've probably got visitors.'

'Well, what about it?' said Japhet. 'They can help. Make a chain gang down the road.'

'My dear boy,' said Louisa, 'can you see Mrs Carter tottering along here on those high heels with a pail of water?'

She smiled grimly; the Carters were a rather alarming joke: their house was so perfect, so shining and spotless, that it looked like one of those television advertisements for the latest magic floor polish. And the Carter children wore special slippers for running round indoors, and other slippers for the bedrooms, and sandals for the garden, and beach shoes for the lake, and of course Wellington boots if there was the slightest sign of rain. The Carters had a lobby where all this footwear was lined up on racks behind a brocade curtain; and Mrs Carter wore spiky heels, or gold embroidered ballet shoes specially for watching television. Mr Carter was something in the City, and went off every day in one of their three cars, wearing dove-grey striped trousers, black jacket, and, of course, a bowler hat. At week-ends the Carters often had parties, and the children then wore hand-smocked dresses and passed round plates of tiny things on sticks.

In the summer, Louisa and Rose went about at home barefoot, so did Japhet, unless he had on his frogman's flippers. Their feet got very dirty, but they could run easily on the roughest gravel path, which made them feel superior to the Carter children, though in some ways they were envious too. Louisa couldn't imagine the Carters having a ceiling fall down *and* a pipe burst, in two days.

'The Gillingses said there used to be a well here,' she said half-heartedly. 'But I suppose it's all filled up.'

'Where? In the garden?' Japhet brightened.

'Where d'you think, dear boy, the pantry? – And that's my *bathing* towel you've been using! Really!'

'O.K., I've finished with it now.' Japhet threw it across to her. Oats shook himself, his ears flapping loudly.

'Honestly, he is the limit,' grumbled Louisa, screwing up her face at the black and smelly towel. Japhet had gone.

It's amazing how much you miss water, Louisa thought later that day. At dinner, the vegetables had tasted most peculiar: it turned out that Rose had been sailing her yacht in one of the buckets.

'I only put a *bit* of soap powder on,' she protested, 'and that didn't work, so –'

'– So you emptied in half a packet, I should think.' Louisa pushed her cabbage to one side.

'Ugh!' Japhet sat with his mouth half open and a

very red face. 'Can I spit it out?'

'Yes, but not in here.'

'Anyway, you'll be deep down clean,' said their mother, and opened a tin of baked beans, which they liked much better than cabbage anyway.

'What on *earth* is Japhet doing?' Louisa looked out of the kitchen window as they were trying to wash up in two inches of water, plus what had been poured off the potatoes. Outside, Japhet appeared to be digging up the back grass. Rose was helping with a trowel from her Junior Gardener's Kit.

'We're digging for that well,' he called. '– Come on, Rosie, mind the fork.' When they were alone together, he was very nice to Rose.

'Put that down at once, that's my best garden fork,' their father shouted. 'Haven't I told you not to take the tools out of the shed?' Japhet and Rose looked at each other and sighed.

'It's like when I tried to dig through to – where was that place?'

'Australia?'

'Yes. By the dustbins at our other house. And then I had to go in to tea, and then after that it was too dark.'

'You never would have got there,' Japhet said.

'You really have dug a lot. Can I stand in it?'

'Yes, if you like. Wouldn't it be funny if there really was a well there, and you disappeared?'

But Rose didn't, so Japhet got into the hole too, and they made a camp there for the rest of the afternoon, scooping out a corner for a kitchen, where they put broken biscuits on rhubarb leaves. Japhet got some fag-ends from an ash-tray, and stuck them on match-sticks so that they could pretend to smoke, but when the end of the matchstick began to burn it made a smell, and Rose choked and wanted a glass of water.

'Your father and Louisa have gone to fetch some more,' said their mother. 'What's left in the kettle is warm.'

'Have milk,' said Japhet. He always suggested that; it was his favourite drink – he said it was good for athletes. His mother often found half-empty bottles in odd places such as the drawing-room fireplace, near the TV, or in his box of electric train things. But Rose disliked milk, so he gave her a huge pat on the back instead. This only made her worse, and she ran indoors spluttering, with a scarlet face and streaming eyes.

Japhet surveyed his afternoon's work, and thought it was a pity that he couldn't try digging in just one other place; the well must be somewhere near the house. The more he looked, the more of a pity he thought it was. After all, he could cover it up quite easily. And the coast was clear, for the moment. And imagine the fun of hearing the prongs of the fork go chink against the stone top of a well. And then they'd all be grateful to him, and when they weren't using the well any more, he could have it for himself, to let things down on the large crane, or fill his water pistol when they wouldn't let him keep coming to the kitchen tap. He might even get an old kettle and make well-water tea on the bon-fire. He never drank tea really, but that would be different.

By the time he had thought all this, Japhet was armed with the fork again; his father had hung it up behind the big garden roller that the children were on no account allowed to push. It had just been bought second-hand from the cricket club, and was very heavy indeed.

Japhet started to dig, this time more quickly and rather wildly. The others might come back at any minute. He guessed that the top of the well couldn't be very far below ground-level, so he didn't bother to make any more deep holes; only a network of shallow troughs, until the back grass looked like a miniature field for tank-practice. The sun beat on his back and shoulders, but he kept in mind the vision of that cool, mossy well; the iron ring he would heave up; the smell of underground dampness; the dark drop and the plop of the first pebble he threw in.

No good; he was caught. His father and mother both closed in on him together, and there was a hot and indignant scene, with Louisa and Rose hanging about in the background looking sober. Finally, Japhet was told to clear it all up.

He looked round. He hadn't realised he had scraped up quite so much earth, and he was tired.

'Will somebody help me?'

'Of all the cheek!' said Louisa. '*I* didn't do it. Besides, I've carried all that water.'

'Is Derek coming tomorrow?' Japhet asked.

'I don't know – why? Oh, of course, it's your half-term,' their mother sighed. 'Yes, I suppose he will, then.'

Derek was the son of Mrs Till, the help who came twice a week. He and Japhet went to the village school. When there was a holiday, Mrs Till brought Derek with her, seeing, as she said, that there was no knowing

31

what he might get up to, left alone. – Or *not* alone, thought Japhet's mother.

'He could help. He likes gardening.'

'D'you call that gardening?' squeaked Rose. 'I should have called it *un*gardening.'

'Anyway,' said their father, 'it's one way of spending half term.'

'They've got a whole week,' said their mother despairingly.

'It's not fair!' Louisa and Rose called out, almost together.

'Well, you get longer real holidays,' Japhet retorted. '*And* taken to all sorts of theatres.'

'Once, to *Midsummer Night's Dream*,' Louisa said. 'In Regent's Park. And it rained.'

Louisa and Rose went to 'that fancy school', as Japhet called it; it was the local High School, but the buildings were more like a College – very dignified red brick, with the lawns kept carpet-smooth. There was a chapel with real stained-glass windows, and the girls had to walk there in absolute silence, two by two, wearing their berets. Japhet and Derek had sometimes spent an odd minute or so comparing all this with *their* school. The barn-like classrooms, the patch of iron-railinged asphalt where they went mad from eleven till eleven-fifteen; the Head Teacher's office, more like a large pantry or a small kitchen; the dark green paint that hardly showed up ink-squirts – their school, they thought, was sensible. That is, if you must have a school at all.

'Anyway,' said their father, 'now that we've got some water, let's have tea.'

They sat on the lawn under the apple-tree. Rose's dolls leaned against a huge branchy lavender-bush; Japhet lay on his stomach putting matches to his piece of sealing-wax and pretending to drip it on the bread-and-butter; Louisa lay stretched on a deck-chair and absent-mindedly ate a whole plate of malt loaf. Their mother sewed the new feather on the hat.

Over the hedge, across the grass, was the road where the week-end cars flashed to and from the coast; the red and yellow and chromium coaches full of hot pink people; the cyclists bent double as they toiled back from their day out. Perhaps some of them glanced aside and envied the family in the garden.

'A six-letter word meaning hot?' asked their father, but got no reply. Japhet was thinking what he would do next day with Derek, and then there were those cuttings to puzzle about. They had obviously been taken from newspapers methodically, for some good reason. He considered asking Louisa about them, but on second thoughts, she might go and bag them for herself. Better to do them up in a packet, fastened up privately with that sealing-wax. One day they might be very valuable, though he couldn't for the moment think why. Anyway, he would keep them to himself.

Louisa was pondering in much the same way about the Captain. A few hours ago it had seemed a brilliant idea, to look for him. Now, she wasn't so sure. She might, perhaps, ask her friend Georgie, at school. But Georgie was apt to be very keen on something for a week, and then drop it. Louisa knew that this would take months – perhaps years, though on a golden summer evening nobody could look ahead as far as that.

Suppose I gave myself a time limit, she thought: say a year; no, say until the end of the summer holidays – and if I haven't got anywhere by then, give it up. But at the very words 'give it up', the day seemed suddenly dead. Once she had set her mind on something, Louisa would go on with it through thick and thin.

'But what shall I do with him when I find him?' she asked herself. The answer to that was such a blank that she decided to leave it until the time came. Meanwhile, she must make a list of possible plans. An idea suddenly struck her: wasn't there something called the Missing Persons Bureau? She wasn't sure of the name, but there was certainly Somerset House, where you looked up births and deaths. . . .

The first thing was to find out the Captain's full name. She immediately worked out exactly how much earlier she would have to start cycling to school if she were to call on the Gillingses again in the morning. And coming right down to earth, she went to make sure that her bicycle hadn't got a puncture; and to count out her money in case she ever wanted it for the fare to London.

She had nine and eightpence halfpenny. She looked up the fare in the ABC. It was six shillings – for a child, and Louisa still passed as this.

'Oh well,' she said to herself firmly, 'so far, so good. It's not very far, but if you don't start in a small way, you don't start at all.'

And she dreamed, that night, of the Captain's dew-wet rocking chair.

Chapter Four

Now meet the pony.

It may seem strange that we haven't mentioned her before – but then, she was rather a strange pony. Her name was Jo, and she had come from a Society that collected old or lame or ailing ponies, and found good homes for them. The field at the back of the children's house was now Jo's good home.

'At any rate, she'll keep the grass down,' their father said. And Jo had started to do this the minute she stepped out of her horse-box. That was in April; it was now June, and Jo had peacefully eaten her way through the worst of the high weeds, so that Rose could now walk across the field with her head showing the whole time.

'*When* shall we be able to ride her?' they kept asking impatiently. 'Fancy having a pony and not riding it!'

This did seem odd, certainly, but there were several reasons – one good, one moderate, and one not so good.

The good reason was that the man who brought Jo said she suffered from something called 'summer itch'. This would come on more in the hot weather, he said, and specially if the grass was very rich. Rich it certainly was, after a wet spring and with no-one else to eat it. And sure enough, Jo's back developed nasty raw pink patches, where the flies clustered to torment her; you couldn't have put a saddle on her in that state.

And anyway, they hadn't got a saddle. This was the not-so-good reason, or so they all thought – though their father pointed out that even a second-hand saddle and bridle cost at least ten pounds.

'But after all,' they argued, 'we got the *pony* for nothing.'

'She's not really ours,' their mother said; 'she's a foster-pony.'

'But what's the good, if we can't ride her?'

Then their father would mumble 'one day', or 'we must see', adding in a louder voice that as far as he was concerned, the pony was saving six pounds a year for getting the grass cut.

'But if she's *saving* us money, then surely——' Japhet would begin, only to be cut short by Louisa, who knew better when to stop an argument, and knew, too, that her father was very short of money since they had come to live in this house. There had been a lot of things to be done, such as having a new chimney put on – and now that ceiling.

'Why don't you ride her bareback?' Derek asked. The answer was the moderately good reason that they couldn't. Apart from the summer itch, Jo was not at all an easy pony to lay your hands on, however much you coaxed. In spite of her age, she had a wild sideways roll in her eye. Just as you thought you had sidled up in a casual enough way to gain her trust, this roll would come, she would snatch the bunch of sweet grass from your hand and gallop off at a speed surprising for an old lady who in pony years was reckoned to be seventy-five. And the man from the Society had said she shouldn't gallop, anyway, because she was broken-winded. So, to Louisa's disappointment, there was no question, yet, of having your photograph taken with your arm flung carelessly round Jo's neck; still less of leaping on her broad bare back.

So Jo just went on eating.

On this hot Monday morning, with the milk already warming by the back door, Jo was peacefully munching clover and moon-daisies as usual when Japhet came out in his Hollywood T-shirt. (An uncle had sent this; it had a picture of palm trees on the front, and Japhet had put it on to impress Derek).

He strolled over to the barbed wire and tore up a fistful of grass; Jo wandered up and nuzzled it greedily out of his hand.

'More?' said Japhet. Jo stuck her head forward and waited. Japhet watched her eating the second and third tufts, and thought how strong she looked, and how strange it was that all that solid muscle should come from just grass. When you thought how their mother was always on about eating up your meat, cheese, eggs, fish . . . it might be all nonsense made up by shop-keepers, wanting you to spend money. Japhet wondered how grass would taste chopped up in milk, and eaten with sugar, like cornflakes.

Then Derek's bus arrived.

Mrs Till hurried up the path with her busy, anxious walk; Derek came behind her, kicking a stone and grinning. Mrs Till always tried to dress him up nice and clean for these visits; the result was a sign of the struggle

37

that must have gone on before they came. Derek had on a perfectly clean blue shirt and spotless white tennis shoes; but between these was a pair of once navy jeans, now slate-coloured, encrusted with dried mud and daubs of green paint. His hair, which when he started off had been plastered down with water, now hung as usual in straight dark spikes all round his face, like pine needles. His eyes were almost black, and he had a chip off a front tooth.

'That's the kind of thing Derek does,' Japhet told Louisa admiringly, 'ride cows'.

'You mean try to,' Louisa said. 'Poor cow – he jolly well deserved to fall off.'

'Did he put the piece of tooth under his pillow,' Rose wanted to know, '– and get sixpence? Or perhaps the fairies would only put threepence, or twopence –'

'Fairies!' said Japhet disgustedly. 'Anyway, I bet you couldn't even get *on* a cow,' he added to Louisa, 'let alone fall off.'

But this morning the girls were safely away at school; Japhet and Derek had the place to themselves. And Japhet's mother decided to go shopping; she wouldn't be able to do it in the afternoon because of the school play. Mrs Till told Derek to behave himself, and mind and not dirty up that shirt. Japhet's mother said if the water-men came, to tell them to get on; the same with the ceiling-men.

Neither lot came. 'They never do,' said Mrs Till, and asked the boys to go and fill a couple of buckets. This took a long time, because they tried that trick of swinging them round, full, right up and over with straight arms. They did this several times.

'Anyway, that can count as washing my hair,' said Japhet. Derek took off his shirt and hung it over a bush in the sun.

'It's her fault for making me wear it,' he said.

'How do you get so brown? Don't you ever peel?'

'No,' said Derek carelessly. 'I just strip to do the pigs, that's all. We had another litter last night. I was out there till half past eleven. Fifteen, she had. Of course, she may have lain on a few by now.'

Japhet looked at him with wonder and respect. Derek's father worked and lived on a farm where they had seven hundred pigs. Derek would help there as soon as he left school. And the sooner the better, he said – he didn't even want to try for a place in the Grammar School.

'Waste of time.' – And he would go on to boast about his latest adventures in pig-rearing. Japhet realised that it was boasting; all the same, he was impressed. Derek had a casual, bitten-off way of talking, in imitation of some of the farm hands. He was tough. Sometimes he didn't answer when you spoke to him; just chewed grass and looked across the field. He really preferred pigs to people, and thought talking was only a way of letting people know how pigs were getting on. He was mildly interested in Jo, but thought it was ridiculous not to ride her.

'I'll break her in for you if you like,' he once said airily. Japhet said Jo was old enough to be broken in already; privately he thought Derek was swanking.

'Well, I could get her on to a leading-rein,' said

Derek, knowing quite well that they didn't possess one.

'We can't even get the halter on her,' Japhet said. 'There it is; you try.'

But Derek just looked at the rope that hung on the gatepost, and chewed a straw.

'When she's eaten the best of the grass,' he said, 'she'll be tamer. Easier to handle.'

So Jo just went on eating.

'We've got to clear this up,' Japhet said. Derek eyed the upheaval of the back grass; he walked slowly round it, like a farmer inspecting his acres. No comment; no question about how it had happened; simply 'Hm. Job for a roller'.

'We can't, it's too heavy.'

'Let's see.'

'– Besides, we're not to.'

'Hm. Might shift it, the two of us,' said Derek, with his bottom lip jutting out and his hands in his pockets as he surveyed the huge roller in the corner of the shed. He gave it a kick, stubbed his toe through his tennis-shoe, but only said 'Come on, let's try.'

They took one side of the handle each and gave a mighty pull. The roller started to move towards them. In fact, as the shed was on a slight slope, it actually rolled towards the door before they could stop it – and there it stuck, jammed against one of the uprights.

After a great deal of hot heaving, they managed to free it; gently, like some monster ambling out of its lair, it came through the opening.

'Now,' said Derek.

'Now,' said Japhet.

But the earthworks ran almost up to the door, and although the roller could be made to trickle downhill, it certainly wouldn't go up, over even the shallowest slope.

'It's no good,' panted Japhet. 'We'd better get the spades. There's that big hole to fill in, anyway.' They looked at it. 'What about elevenses?' said Japhet.

But Mrs Till told them it was only half past nine, and not to come treading on her floor.

'And where's your shirt?' she said.

'I took it off,' said Derek, and went out again.

'Listen!' said Japhet. 'I've got an idea! Let's make Jo pull! She's terrifically strong, I'm sure. If only we could just get the halter on, just this once, and then stick another rope round the handles – the clothes line. . . .'

Derek said nothing, but sauntered towards the barbed wire.

'Jo!' he called. 'Come on, girl!' Japhet knew, then, that he must think it really was a good idea. He was pleased, and started to pull up great handfuls of grass. Jo plodded over, a little suspicious, as she always seemed when there was more than one person – but far from suspecting the truth. Derek took the halter off the gate.

'Let me,' said Japhet, 'it was my idea.'

'Half a minute. Give her some grass. I'll go round the other side.'

He ducked under the barbed wire; Jo's nearest eye began to roll. Japhet impatiently held out the grass – he wished he had taken the halter first.

'Now!' Derek pounced, flinging the halter over the pony's nose; Jo gave a wild glare, and was off with a snort, knocking Japhet full length.

'Let's have another go,' said Derek. 'I'll round her off.' And he started to stalk across the field.

'It's no good,' said Japhet, 'we'll just have to wait for her. Once she's nervous, she won't let you get near.'

His point was proved when Jo, catching sight of Derek pretending to walk carelessly towards her, charged off across the little bridge their father had made, and crashed into the wood.

'Come on,' said Japhet, 'we'd better get the spades or there'll be a fuss.'

They worked away, sweating, for about ten minutes. They had filled in Japhet's hole when Derek said 'it *must* be eleven now.' But it was only ten. They tried the roller again: hopeless. They sat down on it, one each side, and Derek brought out a squashed grey crumpled paper bag.

'What are they?'

'Sherbet things. Only they fell out of my pocket last night and Fancy lay on them.'

'Who's Fancy?'

'The sow. Bit squashed, but still.'

'She must have lain on the fizz,' Japhet said.

'Well, she's one of the biggest we've got,' said Derek. 'I was lucky to get these back, really.'

'Do pigs like sherbet?'

'They like anything.'

'Imagine giving a sherbet dab to a pig!' said Japhet, and started to laugh. 'I bet it'd eat the dab part first, then it'd have to snuffle up the sherbet straight out of the bag.'

'It'd eat the bag,' said Derek seriously. A deep difference between them was that Japhet thought even the word 'pig' was funny; Derek didn't see anything to laugh about in pigs at all; after all, they were his future.

'Look! Quick!' Japhet pointed to the field gate. Jo had come back, and was standing there quietly.

'Tell you what,' said Derek, 'we'll open the gate, just a bit, and let her half-way through, and then hold her so she can't get one way or the other – *then* we can get the halter on.'

'Perhaps, you mean,' said Japhet; but Derek was already unlooping the chain from the gatepost.

Jo watched. Japhet gingerly picked up the halter, which had fallen close by. Jo's eyes began to roll; she stamped the ground, but didn't move away.

'Open the gate a bit more,' Japhet said; 'I'll keep the halter out of sight.'

Derek had to lift the gate where it stuck in the long grass. It hadn't been opened for months.

'Let her think she's going through, then we can –' but Derek said no more.

For Jo didn't only think – she went. Derek was shoved aside; Japhet found himself sitting hard on a thistle. And Mrs Till looked out of the sitting-room window just in time to see the pony go trampling past over the marigolds, gathering speed as she headed for the road.

Japhet and Derek rushed out to the front of the house. Jo gave them one last look, and started to trot across the grass verge. On the main road, she broke into a canter. A car shot by. She reared, turned, crossed the ditch, and galloped straight over the cricket pitch, on to the common and out of sight into the bracken beyond.

'*Now* what've you been and gone and done?' cried Mrs Till.

They looked at each other, aghast.

And believe it or not, at that very minute a small grey car drew up by the white posts that marked the way in from the road, and a man in a cap stepped out.

'That'll be for the water,' said Mrs Till. 'One thing after another!'

But Japhet's heart sank with horror into what would have been his boots if he hadn't had bare feet; he recognised the man from the Pony Society.

'Anyone at home, sonny? Just come to have a look at your pony – we always make a point of inspecting after the first three months. How's she doing – all right, is she? Summer itch come on yet?'

'A bit,' muttered Japhet.

'Well, let's go and have a look-see, shall we?'

Japhet stood speechless as the man strode cheerfully towards the empty field.

Chapter Five

When Japhet's mother came back, the pony man was sitting in the kitchen, drinking his second cup of tea in grim silence.

'I shall have to make a report about this,' he said. 'I'm afraid the committee will take a serious view. Even *should* you recover the animal, I very much doubt if we could agree to let you keep her.'

Japhet's mother said she quite understood, but this might be a lesson to them; it would never happen again.

'That's not the question, madam. Once is too often. Of course, should the animal *not* be recovered, or be found in a bad condition, you realise you are liable –'

'Yes, yes, we should have to pay, of course,' and she looked at Japhet, who thought of the money he had saved up for a level-crossing.

'You say she went that way,' said the man, as they walked miserably out to his car. Japhet nodded.

'There are gipsies over there,' he said. They might help. They're used to horses.'

The man looked sour. 'I'll take the car and have a squint round, though I'm overdue at my next call as it is. – A *very* good home,' he added pointedly, '– they've had one of our animals for ten years. Have you got the halter we provided?'

Japhet ran to fetch it, relieved at having something to do.

'She's not shod, either,' the man went on. 'She's no business on the roads at all. May damage her feet badly.'

'It was across the common she galloped,' Japhet's mother said weakly. 'That's quite soft.'

'Galloped, eh? She's got no business to be galloping,' snapped the man.

Derek opened his mouth to say something, but Mrs Till dragged him off to the bus stop. It had suddenly occurred to her that if he was mixed up in this, and there was something to pay, it might be as well to be out of the way.

'Wait till your Dad hears, he'll give you a piece of his mind,' she said.

'. . . Whatever your father will say, I can't think,' Japhet's mother was saying at the same time. Then she went to phone the police, and some neighbouring houses; Japhet didn't dare to ask for dinner.

Nor did he dare to think what the girls would say, specially Louisa.

What was more, he couldn't get the roller back into the shed.

In despair he went and drank a whole bottle of milk.

Meanwhile, Louisa was hoping to goodness her mother wouldn't be late for the play – and that she would wear the small white hat, not the pink pudding-basin everyone had stared at last year. She wished she had remembered to mention this.

By lunch-time the costume was laid out ready in the games pavilion, which was to be the dressing-room. Out on the field stood the painted hut which was the school's prize dramatic property, and came out in every possible play. The roses round the door had been touched up for the occasion by the Art mistress, and the chimney sprouted a huge wad of cotton-wool smoke, stuck on inside with adhesive tape. In the doorway of this hut Louisa was to sit, telling the story of the play to the audience which would fill the ten rows of metal chairs.

To her great relief, a breeze had sprung up; it fluttered the 'Reserved' notices on the front row, and made the cotton-wool smoke wag like a giant dog's tail.

To her still further relief, she spotted her mother among the reasonably early arrivals – but looking, Louisa thought, rather worried. And without Japhet, who was supposed to have come. Louisa herself was quite anxious, but she did know her part – in fact she knew the whole play, they had rehearsed it so often.

'Now, people, you'll have to speak up even more than usual,' Miss Bleakie told them. 'This is a south-west breeze, so nice loud voices, please! Now, does any girl want doing up? How are our hooks and eyes? That third rosebush, you're coming apart in the middle, dear. Now where are my courtiers? – No, I haven't got a pin, ask Miss Fisk. – One two, only three of you – *where* is Georgia? Well tell her to hurry up, you all had plenty of time to wash . . .'

Oh dear, thought Louisa, she's making us even more nervous than we really are. In the distance, she saw one of the mother's hats blow off, and go spinning across the field towards the tennis courts.

The play started with Louisa telling the story of two children who were supposed to be lost in the wood.

Whether they ever got found again was beside the point. The boy was Edwina Beale, small and skinny with glasses; she had been chosen because of her short straight hair and enormous voice. The girl-child was Lucy Tavistock, who always got 'pretty' parts without much to say. She was dainty-looking but rather a mouse. Louisa, especially with her high hat and feather, towered above them both. She saw Georgia arriving, puffed, from the cloakrooms, holding up her red and black courtier's skirt and showing large brown sandals and white socks underneath.

'My dear child, where are your slippers?' cried Miss Bleakie. Georgia said somebody must have taken them by mistake. Her dark pigtails were wound up under a butter-muslin wimple; she looked quite stately, not at all as if she would pass you a potato crisp in Latin, let alone flip the little blue bag of salt right across the room off the end of a ruler, to land it neatly on Miss Congreave's woolly grey head – so woolly that there it had stayed, and poor Connie hadn't known what was the matter with them all. . . .

The rows of chairs were full; the headmistress had arrived, to sit in the place of honour in front. There was a tittering scuttle in the laurel bushes behind the 'stage' as the forest animals, played by juniors, got into line. These juniors had been chosen simply for the costumes they could provide; there was a chicken, a cat, two rabbits, several butterflies and moths, and a penguin. (The penguin was new that term; Miss Bleakie had let her be in it to cheer her up, because she was apt to cry at break.)

The upright piano, dragged down to the field by the

48

beetly-looking school gardener and his assistant, struck up with the opening music. The play had begun.

Louisa sat squarely on her stool, with one of her father's old pipes in her mouth, pretending to shave pieces of wood off a tent-peg with a knife from the Domestic Science room. She had been shaving away at this tent-peg every day for weeks; if the knife had been sharp, there would have been no peg left by now. She didn't know what she was supposed to be making but it gave her something to do with her hands.

All went well until the beginning of scene two. This was where Georgia came in with the other courtiers; they were out hunting. Behind the laurel bushes, Jane Tindale puffed her cheeks to give a mighty blast on the horn borrowed from somebody's brother. There came a tiny broken squeak, ending downhill. Georgie started to giggle.

'So the king's hunt rode royally through the forest,' Louisa had to say, but wondered if she should wait for Jane to try again.

She was not long wondering – for at that moment, the breeze, which had turned to a real wind, blew with a tremendous gust. There was a cracking, a flapping of plywood, and the hut lurched sideways, belched outwards, and then lifted off the ground, roses and all, and heeled over to land in a broken shambles some yards away. The chimney, with the cotton-wool, sailed off separately into a hawthorn tree.

There was a gasp, and cries of dismay from the mothers, who were all holding their hats.

'So the king's hunt. . . .' Louisa began stalwartly, sitting exposed on the steps and holding her hat too.

But this was one of the times when the show couldn't go on, though she had always been told it must. Miss Bleakie, in consternation, rushed out from the bushes, book in hand, making frantic signs to some sixth-form girls who were waiting in the background to organise the silver collection.

They started to pick up the pieces. The courtiers, now in fits of laughter, came forward uncertainly to help, but Miss Bleakie shoved them fiercely off-stage. Lucy, the 'little girl', sat blinking stupidly, with a weak smile on her face. Edwina took out her spectacles, which she had been told not to wear for the play, and gazed at the wreckage with solemn surprise.

And what should Louisa do? It flashed through her mind that she might make up some lines, such as 'But there was a storm in the forest that day . . .' or 'Come, my children, we will go on with the story another time . . .' But the audience had started talking, and there was such an atmosphere of flurry that she would not be heard anyway, and it would look as if she had just panicked.

So she decided to smoke her pipe. Muttering 'Stay there!' to the two dazed 'children', she sucked away, trying to look peaceful, and gazing straight ahead over the mothers' hats as though she were looking placidly at a pleasant view. And there she sat, while the hut was reconstructed round her, from behind – though minus chimney – and Miss Bleakie told the sixth-form girls to stay and hold the walls in place. Louisa wondered if she ought to take some dramatic interest in all this, but thought it best to sit as if nothing had happened.

'Well,' she announced at last, giving the audience a comforting and sympathetic smile, 'well –' and she knocked out her pipe against the swaying doorway – 'So the king's hunt rode royally through the forest. . . .'

Her friends told her afterwards that she had saved the situation.

'How on earth did you manage not to laugh?' said Georgia. 'I should have burst!'

'It wouldn't have been any good, bursting,' Louisa said.

'Even Miss Bleakie was in a flap!'

'You can't be in a flap sitting down,' said Louisa.

What she didn't mention was the one thought that had really helped: the thought of the Captain. It had suddenly come to her: that was how he must have felt, sitting there high and dry with no house. His hadn't blown away, but he had sat, like her, among his bare furniture. And she was sure he would have smoked a pipe, and looked across the common as she had looked over the mothers' heads – though while he would have puffed, furicus real smoke, she was only acting.

His name, the Gillingses had told her early that morning, was Noah Fogwill.

'Are you sure about the Noah?' It was all the more odd when she had a brother called Japhet.

'Noah was the name,' said Mr Gillings.

'– Though whatever she wanted to come and ask for, I can't imagine,' Mrs Gillings said afterwards. '– Bringing that little Rose all this way round on their bikes, they're comical children and that's a fact.'

'I dare say we was as comical once,' said Mr Gillings, and went on hoeing round his lettuces.

And all that afternoon, Japhet had been scouring the common and the lanes for Jo.

He took an apple in each pocket, and, on second thoughts, some biscuits, and on third thoughts a handful of sultanas for iron rations. He fetched those old newspapers, done up with tape and sealing-wax, and stuffed them into his shorts, in case anyone should break in and steal them. The sealing-wax made them look specially valuable. They stuck rather far out of his pocket, and he couldn't get them inside his shoe, as spies did on television, so in the end he went down the road with a curious bulge in front of his T-shirt. He locked the back door, put the key on the ledge, and took Oats with him.

He came back hot and dusty, still with the bulge, but without the apples, biscuits, sultanas, Oats – or Jo.

'Stupid dog,' he grumbled, 'just because of a rabbit . . .'

But Louisa and Rose were not able even to think about Oats; the loss of Jo was too much of a disaster for the nicest garden tea to be any pleasure. Rose cried and wouldn't eat. Louisa grumbled furiously about boys, and said she hoped Derek would never be allowed to come again. Their mother flitted about with her hair on end, telephoning, cutting herself with the bread-knife, fetching buckets of water because Mrs Till had used the last drop.

Their father came home hot and tired, and was very much annoyed. He said Japhet had better start saving up his money, and as for the dog, he wished they had never had him. Japhet was waiting to be blown up about the garden roller, but no-one noticed it.

Oats slunk back just as they were going to bed. He was covered in burrs from head to paw; Louisa set about pulling them off, since no-one else would.

Later, she lay awake thinking how horrible it would be if they really had to give Jo back. Now we've got two things to find, she thought, and had a crazy vision of the Captain clopping across the common on Jo's back. . . .

Rose at last went peacefully to sleep with the long feather on her pillow. Her mother had told her that they would be sure to find Jo somewhere, some time, perhaps in the morning; and Rose would always believe her mother, in the end. . . .

Japhet wondered whether he might sell his papers to a museum for an enormous sum. Or better still, whether there was something else up there under that ceiling – some real treasure. There was a trap-door in the landing, outside the bathroom. If he were to get up there tomorrow he could surely worm his way along the beams and explore. It could do no harm, and even if he sold his electric train, there wouldn't be enough to pay for Jo. . . .

So the three children slept. Little did they know what was happening out in the garden.

Chapter Six

Japhet got up first, in spite of its being his holiday. He always woke early; there was a house-martins' nest under the eaves just outside his bedroom window, and their breakfast noises were shrill.

He went downstairs in his pyjamas to get some milk. Oats, still sleepy, lazily propped his sooty chin over the side of his basket. Japhet stood with bare feet on the cool brick floor, enjoying the coldness of the milk and the feeling that he needn't get dressed for ages – and even then, he could wear his bathing trunks if he wanted to. It was going to be another hot day. Just the kind for sitting under the hose, and squirting it high so so that the water fell straight out of the sky on to your head. But of course, there was no water.

– And no Jo, Japhet remembered. How ever could he have forgotten it for a moment?

He went to the kitchen window, in the wild hope that he might see her feeding quietly outside. But no. He wondered if, with some giant effort, he could at least get that roller back into the shed before the others came down.

He looked towards the shed – then he looked again. His mouth dropped open; his blue eyes went as round as glass marbles.

The roller had gone! – At least, that was what he

thought at first – but when he opened the window and peered out more closely, he saw that it hadn't gone – it had sunk!

There, sprouting out of the earth, was its iron handle, slightly askew and just on a level with what remained of the back grass.

He rushed out, followed by Oats, who had now shaken his ears enough to flap himself awake.

Together they stood and stared, Japhet with his toes curled into the edge of crumbled earth, Oats blowing excited snuffs through his nose, and prancing round the hole like a mad creature.

'The well!' Japhet gasped. 'Oats, we've found the well!'

And Oats wagged what would have been his tail – which meant that the whole of his back end twitched and wriggled and worried the air with joy.

Sure enough, the roller must have stood right over the opening. And its enormous weight, during the night, had made the earth subside, and had splintered through the rotted wooden top of the well. This top, Japhet judged, had been about a foot below the grass; it was all that kept the thing from caving in. Not that this would ever have happened, with people just walking ordinarily across – but never before, probably, had it had anything so heavy standing right over it for so long.

And now the roller had stuck in the mouth of the well, wedged against the brick sides and partly held up by the wood that had broken downwards and inwards. There were still some pieces dragged down but not broken right off; they stuck under the roller like split grey claws. The narrowness of the brickwork had stopped it from falling further; Japhet saw that as it was, you'd have a job to move it one way or the other, it was so tilted and jammed.

He knelt down, pyjamas and all, and stared through the gap between the curve of the roller and the side of the well. Pitch dark, no knowing how deep it was. He dropped a clod of earth down, and waited for the splash. Nothing – only a light thump. So the well must be dry.

This was very disappointing; to have got the roller stuck in a wet well might have been forgiven; to have landed it in a dry one was only going to make people furious.

Still, perhaps it might fill up again . . . Japhet was always an optimist. After all, the ditch by the wood was dry, with all this hot weather; they had to fill Jo's old zinc bath every day. . . .

'And perhaps there's buried treasure down there!'

Oats gazed up hopefully.

'– Or some clue the police have been wanting for years!'

Oats did his best to grin.

'– Or something to do with those papers, that'd unsolve the mystery and lead to a secret fortune!'

Oats looked impressed, and waited for more.

But really, at the back of Japhet's mind, and prodding steadily to the front, for all his hopes, was one certain fact: in a few minutes there was going to be a terrible fuss. When you had been told not to touch a roller at all, it looked even worse to get it stuck in a well. That was all people would think: it wouldn't occur to them to be pleased.

It didn't.

'This is the last straw,' his father said.

'And anyway, I *hate* wells,' his mother added unexpectedly. 'A girl I used to play with fell into one and broke both arms.'

'*Both* arms!' Rose was interested at once.

'Or both legs, I can't remember – anyway, two things. They covered that well up and sealed it down then, and a good job too. All wells should be sealed down.'

Japhet went upstairs muttering that not even a baby could fall into this well, at the moment; if they felt like that about it, they'd better leave the roller there and be thankful: he might have saved all their lives.

The only one who took his side at all was Rose. She went out to look, and had to be hauled in to finish her breakfast. Then she went out again, and accidentally dropped a very small celluloid doll called Gretel down between the roller and the bricks.

'The first casualty,' their mother said grimly.

'Anyway,' Louisa tried to comfort Rose, '*she* can't break both arms, because she only had one; the other's in the knife box.'

'She had two legs,' wept Rose, '– and even socks.'

'Really,' sighed Louisa on the way to school, 'everything happens to us.' Rose's face was still tear-stained; at home there seemed to be one mess after another; worst of all, Jo was still astray. Louisa looked over the fields and hedges as she pedalled along; she told Rose to do the same.

But Rose was still thinking about Gretel, and even the chocolate cigar her mother had given her for break didn't help. (Besides, it had been taken out of last year's Christmas decorations, and Rose knew that taste of old chocolate, though she didn't want to seem ungrateful).

Louisa couldn't concentrate on her work at all that day. She told Georgia about her troubles, but all Georgia could say was 'honestly, what rotten luck!' – over and over again, with not a single practical suggestion. In fact Georgia was inclined to give things up for lost too easily, Louisa thought; but then, Georgia had the art of conveniently forgetting one thing and going on to the next. This could be maddening if you were trying to organise, say, a Form Stall for Open Day: Georgia would forget to bring the jam she had promised, but turn up brightly with a wonderful suggestion for decorating the table with crepe paper rosettes, when Louisa had already cut out canvas flags. On the other hand, her short memory made Georgia a good friend, because she never had a grievance or took offence. You could be cross with her before prayers, and she would still be giggling with you in the first lesson, passing you salted peanuts wrapped in drawings of Miss Bleakie.

Rose spent the morning being sad about Gretel; and at break her friends weren't even sympathetic. All they did was boast about the dolls they'd lost at various times, each one bigger and better than the last. This ended in such a quarrel that Rose and another girl had to stand by the staff-room door, one each side of the lost property notice-board.

This board gave Rose an idea.

After school dinner she slipped back into the form-room when she should have been outside; there she carefully tore a page out of her Nature note-book, chose a red from her crayon set, and wrote:

LOST 1 PONEY.

She put her name and form and a red star in each corner; there was no time for more.

There was no-one about; the mistresses were all inside the staff-room having their coffee. She pinned up her notice on the board and ran quickly out to the playground. She felt she had done something very sensible; Louisa would be pleased. Of course it was strictly not allowed, in that school, to tear a page out of a book; but Rose reasoned that ponies were Nature; even Miss Bleakie must understand that.

So much for the girls.

Japhet was watching the water-men, who had dug a trench along the side of the house. One of them was in it, brown with mud; the other rested on his spade and looked on, with a flattened cigarette stuck to his bottom lip.

'Time for a cuppa tea,' he said.

And they went off to lie in the shade of their van, on the grass. There they drank a flask of tea and ate thick white sandwiches, chewing at leisure and talking about the cars that passed by.

Japhet didn't fall into the trench; he sloped round to the kitchen to see what might be going for him. His mother gave him a huge brown crust, roughly buttered, and told him to go away. She still seemed pretty fed up, he thought.

He went to have another look at the roller. The water-men had said it would need a crane: Japhet very much looked forward to seeing a crane in his garden. Even Derek would be impressed; they didn't have cranes for pigs. At the very thought of that word, Japhet started to grin, and felt more cheerful.

'I'm going out,' his mother told him, 'to make some more inquiries about that pony. If anyone calls about her tell them to wait. If the water-men want anything, let them in. If the phone rings, write a message on the pad. There's plenty of milk.'

And she went off in the elderly car, with the hood down and a piece of sacking hanging out of the boot. (This was kept there to cover the hole where the rain sometimes got into the petrol.)

Japhet went straight to that trap door by the bathroom.

He fetched a ladder, and knocked some paint off the banisters, getting it upstairs. But it was just long enough to prod open the trap door and lean against the edge.

He crawled over dark spidery beams. Underneath here would be the bathroom; if he fell through now, he might land in the bath. These beams must be very old; he wondered if any of them might be part of ships' timbers; they did use those for houses sometimes. He had visions at once of finding a salvaged bit of the Spanish Armada, or a piece of Nelson's 'Victory' – but of course that was impossible, unless the one they had at Portsmouth was a fake. Japhet's imagination was just playing with the idea of exposing the naval authorities as a lot of frauds, and being interviewed on TV as The Boy Who Found the *Real* 'Victory'. 'For which he will receive a reward of . . .' etc. etc., when he gave his head a most deadly bang.

He reeled, grabbed for a beam, missed it, and slipped.

Some minutes later, when he came to on Louisa's bedroom floor, he realised that he was very lucky indeed not to have broken anything. But not so lucky to have brought down the little that was left of that ceiling. Plus, he noted, quite a lot of laths. Plus a bird's nest. Plus . . . what was that in the corner? Aching as he was, he crawled across the room and pulled out something from the newly-fallen plaster. He stared, amazed. Turned it over. Heavy. Wiped off some dust with the palm of his hand. Mahogany – the one wood he could recognise. Noticed a small metal plate, blackened but with engraved letters on it: 'The Alberta. 1880.'

It was a ship's compass.

Before he could even begin to wonder how it had come there, there was a knock at the front door, a bang at the back, and the telephone rang, all at the same time. Japhet picked himself up, rubbed as much plaster as possible out of his hair, and went downstairs.

When his mother came back, she found the kitchen full of people.

Sitting at the table, with his helmet on the fridge, was a policeman. One of the water-men protruded from the cupboard under the sink; the other stood by and smoked. On the other side of the table, a large man with a moustache sat with his cap in his hands, chewing. A completely strange boy stood by the back door. And, of all people, the elegant Mrs Carter sat on a third kitchen chair, her grey and white dress spread out like

61

a fan, her high-heeled white sandals neatly crossed, her toe-nails coral-coloured and her hair pale blue.

'Good gracious!' said Japhet's mother. 'I'm so sorry. Don't get up. Which of you was first?'

'O.K. in 'ere,' said a voice from under the sink.

'Just checkin' up,' the other water-man explained.

'About your pony –' the policeman began.

'I'm from the breakdown,' said the man with the moustache.

'I feel I've called at a most terrible time . . .' said Mrs Carter.

'That man from the Pony Society rang up,' Japhet muttered.

The strange boy said nothing at all; he just stood looking dark.

'Would anybody like a cup of tea?' said Japhet's mother desperately. 'How many are there? One, two, three. . . .' She put out seven cups and saucers, taking care that Mrs Carter got one that was not chipped.

'I never can refuse tea, isn't it awful!' simpered Mrs Carter.

'You need a wet, this weather,' said the water-man with the cigarette.

'Same 'ere,' mumbled the voice from the sink cupboard.

'Well, if you're making it . . .' said the policeman. And the man with the moustache moved whatever he was chewing to the other side, and said thanks very much, as a matter of fact he had a throat, added to which, hot tea was cooling. The boy by the door still said nothing. He looked from one to another of them with interest, as if they were animals in a zoo.

When they were all stirring their cups and eating digestive biscuits (except Mrs Carter, who had to think of her figure), Japhet slipped away to put that ship's compass in his wardrobe. His mother hadn't had time to notice his plastery, dusty condition; he wiped himself with a damp flannel and finished off with a towel, which he replaced on the rail dirty side inwards. He also shut Louisa's door, considering that this was not the best moment to display the broken laths. The ladder was still in place, and he couldn't get it down without being seen, so with much difficulty he dropped it out of the bathroom window, only breaking one rosebush in the flower bed below.

When he got downstairs again, everybody had gone except the strange boy.

'That man's seeing about bringing a crane,' his mother said, '– and Mrs Carter very kindly offered to send along their shooting-brake full of water, they've got a tank or something, but we shan't need it now. Bert promises we can use the taps by tonight.'

'Jack,' said Japhet, 'if you mean the one with the red hair.'

'Anyway, that policeman hasn't found Jo; he wanted further details. – And I shouldn't have called it red,' said his mother, who always talked about several things at once. 'More auburn. – And now,' – turning to the silent boy – 'what can we do for *you*?'

'Was that your pony come over the potato field?' said the boy.

'Where? When? What d'you mean?'

'Brown, with a white nose?'

'Yes, yes – have you seen her?'

'No shoes on 'er?'

'Yes – no – where is she?'

'We got 'er tied up,' said the boy calmly. 'Over our place.'

'But where *is* your place?' Japhet's mother was nearly beside herself.

'Our caravan. Just across the common. My Dad says what'll you take for 'er?'

'Take? She's not for sale: she's not even ours.'

'You just said she was.'

'Well, she's borrowed. We're looking after her.'

The boy looked at her with expressionless black eyes. 'Couldn't you borrow 'er to us? My Dad just wants a pony like that. Pull our cart.'

'I dare say he did, but I'm afraid you can't possibly have her; we're responsible for her. You must ask your Dad please to bring her back at once.'

' 'E's away. Gone strawberry-pickin'.'

'Then can't you or your mother bring her back?'

'Mum's gone to 'ospital with the baby. There's only me and me little brother.'

'But can't *you* bring her back?' asked Japhet. 'You know about ponies, don't you? I thought all gipsies – I mean, I thought you did.'

'Oh, I know about ponies,' said the boy casually. 'That's why we were thinking she'd be just the thing. Couldn't you ask your friends if –'

'No we couldn't!' interrupted Japhet's mother, thinking of that sour little man from the Society. 'But why didn't you say all this when that policeman was here?'

64

For the first time, the boy almost smiled.

'We don't give much for 'im,' he said, 'and 'e's not struck on us either. My Dad says best to keep your mouth shut. Don't want no trouble.'

'You don't consider the trouble *we're* in!' Japhet's mother exclaimed.

' 'Oo come to let 'er out, then?' asked the boy coolly.

Japhet flushed. 'Look here,' he said, 'shall I go round with him and see if she's really all right? – Have you given her water? Has she got grass?'

'See for yourself,' said the boy with a shrug.

Japhet walked with him in silence along the road and across the common; not a word was said until they reached the bushes where the gipsies had settled with two caravans and an old cart.

'It's her!' cried Japhet. 'It's Jo!'

'I said you could see for yourself, didn't I?' said the boy. 'Hi, Danny!' he shouted.

A very dirty white face appeared at the window of the further caravan. Then a small boy in long trousers came out.

'We can't 'ave 'er,' said the older boy.

'Why not?'

'She's not theirs.'

'But Dad said –'

'Shut up, will you?'

'But if she's not theirs –'

'Shut up!' The older boy was furious; it was his bottled-up disappointment coming out. Japhet felt sorry for the smaller boy.

'Perhaps you could come and have a ride on her,' he said. '– When we've got a saddle.' He had quite forgotten that they might not be allowed to keep Jo anyway; the important thing was that she was found.

The smaller boy's face lit up. 'I don't need no saddle,' he said. 'I can ride like at the circus. That's what I'm going to be, one day, a proper circus rider.'

'So you say,' said the older boy rather nastily. ' –'E's a little liar,' he added to Japhet. 'Pony-mad, 'e is. – Rather be chasin' ponies than go to school, wouldn't you, eh?'

'Yes,' said Danny simply.

'Well, you're comin' to school Monday or Dad'll belt you, and if 'e's not there, I will. Now get back in and shut up! Go on, before I give y'a bloody nose!'

Then the older boy turned and stroked Jo's nose most lovingly.

Japhet walked back home wondering, and somewhat disturbed. He had never seen that kind of life at close quarters before. The draggled bushes, the rubbish thrown in the brambles, it was all depressing. Jo seemed safe enough for the time being, and that was a great relief – but what about Danny? Japhet was sometimes horrid to his own sisters; but he was by nature a kindly boy, and even secretly saw himself as something of a Sir Ivanhoe to the poor and downtrodden. Ought not Danny to be rescued? Might that other boy really beat him up? Wasn't there a Society for the prevention of that sort of thing?

But what with cranes and compasses and old wells and mysterious papers to think about, and those laths to explain, Japhet didn't have much time to dwell on Danny. This was a good thing, because, as he was to find out later, he would have been wasting his good will. To know why, you will have to meet Danny on his own; but not quite yet.

Chapter Seven

'Right!'
'Right!'
' 'Eave away!'
'Watch 'er, then'.'
'O.K.'
'Is she shiftin'?'
'Give it another turn – steady! Whoa!'

The man with the moustache, still chewing, and with his cap on the back of his head, was shouting instructions to another man who sat in the lorry and operated the crane.

Louisa, Rose, Japhet and Derek looked on. It was Saturday morning, and Japhet had begged for Derek to be allowed to come and see the fun.

'They won't squash Gretel, will they?' Rose asked anxiously.

Derek eyed the operations critically, pretending he was quite used to this kind of thing.

'They ought to move in,' he said. 'Lorry's too far away. Wrong angle.'

But as he spoke, there was a great grinding of chains, a tremendous rasping of iron against brick – and slowly but surely the roller rose and hung for a moment, a dead weight in the air. Even Derek forgot himself.

'Here she comes! Look out! Stand back!' he shouted.

The man with the moustache straddled the well. There were a lot of 'O.K.s!' and 'Whoas!' as they managed to steady the crane's great burden and set it down on the grass. There it sat, black, bulky and obstinate – almost, Louisa thought, as if it were sulking.

'Where's Gretel?' asked Rose.

'How deep is it?'

'Let's see!'

'Mind out, I want to look too!'

They all crowded round the well; the man with the moustache said 'Now then, you kids, mind what you're a-doin' of; fifty foot drop there, for all you know.'

Japhet knelt down and tried to yodel, whereupon their mother rushed out and said the well was to be covered up at once, or she wouldn't have a moment's peace.

'But where's *Gretel*?' wailed Rose, and at the sight of her father bringing up some heavy pieces of wood, she burst into such a flood of tears that the man with the moustache even stopped chewing.

'What's up? Lost your dollie, 'ave you?' he said kindly. '– Give us the rope, Bill. We'll drop this down first, see 'ow deep it really is. Then if the ladder'll do it. . . .'

They all watched admiringly while he tied a big metal hook to the end of the rope, then lowered it until there was a slight thud and it began to sag.

'That's about the measure of 'im, then,' said the man. 'Not more'n twenty foot. If that. Give us the ladder, Bill.'

'Are you sure it's safe?' asked their mother. The man winked.

'I've got a little girl at 'ome myself,' he said. 'She'd 'ave me down bloomin' Vesuvius if she lost 'er doll. Reckon I'd go an' all,' he grinned. His cap was now level with the ground.

'Well, ta-ta,' he said. 'I'll 'ave forget-me-nots round me grave.' They watched the top of his cap getting darker and darker.

'Hey!' a voice boomed from below. 'Got a light, anybody?'

Japhet raced to get his torch, then remembered that the battery had gone. Louisa fetched her bicycle lamp, and they lowered it on a string.

'You all right?' called Bill, the other man, who didn't much approve of all this.

'What's this 'ere doll like?' said the underground voice.

'Only small,' called Rose, 'with a blue dress and one arm and socks.'

The cap started to rise to the surface again.

'This 'er?' In the palm of his hand lay Gretel, looking even smaller than Rose had remembered, and rather dirty.

'Yes! Thank you, very much.'

'Found something else down there too.'

Japhet's eyes brightened; he tingled with excitement.

'What? Show us.'

'One old boot,' said the man, '– and this.'

And he held out a skull.

'But it's not a person's,' said Japhet, '– is it?'

'A horse?' asked Rose.

'How could a horse fall down a well?' said Louisa.

'He might not've fallen,' said Rose, 'he might've been pushed.' (It was the sort of remark that made Louisa despair.)

'A pig'd be wider,' Derek said.

'Suppose,' suggested Japhet, 'it was a prehistoric animal!'

'Don't be silly, it'd be buried much deeper than that,' Louisa told him.

'Looked a bit pre'istorical down there,' said the man.

'Some boot!' remarked their father, holding up the huge greenish mouldering object. 'Looks like a sea-boot to me.' This was just what Louisa had been thinking.

'I say,' said Japhet, 'can I have that skull?'

'I wasn't thinkin' of puttin' it on me mantelpiece,' smiled the man, and handed it over. Louisa took the boot; Rose was still clutching Gretel.

'I thought it was a proper big doll you'd lost,' said the man. 'Like one of them walkie-talkies.'

'Has your little child got a walkie-talkie?' asked Rose.

'Yes; 'ad it last Christmas. Real nylon 'air an' all; you can wash it.'

'I had a doll with real hair,' said Rose, 'when I was young. But she died.'

'What of?'

'Just age,' sighed Rose. 'She all fell apart.'

' 'Ard cheese,' said the man. 'I always reckon it's 'ard cheese when anybody falls apart.' He seemed really to pity her for setting so much store by a little one-armed doll like Gretel.

' 'Ere,' he said, 'I always carry some of these,' and he gave her a cough sweet, which was quite nice at first but had to be spat out later.

'P'raps I'll be round your way again,' he said. 'I'll look out for you.'

Rose went out to the front and waved him goodbye; she felt she had made a friend.

Their mother and father were busy covering the well – though it would have to be done properly later, with cement.

Rose found Louisa, Japhet and Derek sitting in the chicken house. This was unusual – Louisa generally had very little to do with the boys when they were together, or they with her.

They told Rose she couldn't come in unless she went to fetch the elevenses; so she did. When she got back to the chicken house, Louisa was measuring the old boot with a tape-measure.

'It must be at least size twelve,' she said. 'So he was a very big man. I mean *is*. Anyway, it's a clue.'

The boys sat on the ground, vigorously tapping the compass. The skull and Japhet's bundle of papers lay in a corner.

Too much had happened for either Louisa or Japhet to be able to keep it all to themselves.

'I don't see the point,' said Derek when Louisa had finished telling her story about the Captain.

'I do,' said Japhet. 'He might have a fortune hidden away –'

'Oh, you and your fortunes!' Louisa interrupted him. 'That's not the point at all. The thing is, the poor old man was turned out, so we've got to try to find out what happened to him.'

'Why?' asked Derek.

Louisa flung down the boot in impatience. 'If you can't see that, you can't see anything. – Because it's only decent, it's only fair. Why, he might be starving!'

'Dead, more like,' said Derek.

'Besides,' – Rose had been thinking carefully – 'he might not of.'

'Might not have what, for goodness sake?' Louisa cried.

'Had a fortune hidden away,' said Rose.

'Oh heaven's, we're not talking about that now. And don't take all the fly-biscuits.'

'But it all happened years ago, you said,' persisted Derek.

'Well, what about it? Seamen live to a good old age. You just don't seem to have any feelings.' Louisa was getting more indignant; Derek's dullness was just what she needed to work her up to the good cause. 'Here's this poor lonely old man,' she went on warmly, '– and that's probably his favourite dog' – pointing to the skull – 'that threw itself into the well in despair when it found its master had gone away –'

'It would have picked up the scent,' said Derek.

'– And there's his compass, probably given to him in honour of long and faithful service, and he never even had a chance to come and get it back, because that beastly Mr Glover was always prowling round with the key. Besides,' she finished up, 'even if we didn't find him, we should have tried, and we shouldn't feel so bad about it, and it would have been an adventure.'

72

'Yes,' said Japhet, grasping this last point at once, though he didn't feel bad about anything. 'All right. Where shall we start? – He might let me keep the compass, anyway,' he added. 'Specially if those papers are really valuable.'

Louisa ignored this. 'First I shall find out whether he's still alive,' she said firmly. They asked her how, and she told them about Somerset House, which reduced them to respectful silence until they began to discuss the problem of her getting there.

'Just say you want to go,' said Derek. 'Or just go.' His life must be very simple, Louisa thought.

'In the first place, they wouldn't let me,' she said, 'they'd say it was just a wild goose chase.' (And she would know they were probably right, which would make it worse.) '– And in the second place, we want to keep this a secret. That's half the fun. People'd only laugh if we told them now. So if we don't find him, they need never know; and if we do, think of the thrill of having traced a real live Missing Person, all by ourselves.'

'Or dead,' said Derek.

'What's a wild goose chase?' asked Rose, always one behind.

At that moment who should appear but Jo, led down the path by a very sulky-looking man with a grey scarf that had once been white; it made him seem particularly hot and dirty. Following him was Danny, keeping some yards behind, and wearing a vest, rolled-up trousers and braces.

They rushed to welcome Jo, and led her into the field in triumph. But the gipsy hung around and wanted to talk to their father. He simply wouldn't believe that Jo was not theirs to sell.

'It's not as if you're using her, is it?' he kept saying; 'It's not as if I was asking for a favour. I'm offering a fair price.'

In vain their father told him about the Society, and how Jo was not supposed to be used for work anyway; the gipsy had never heard of such a thing, and he obviously thought it was just a story to do him out of a bargain.

'It's because we're gipsies,' he said, 'that's what it is.'

Danny hung wistfully against the barbed wire, staring at Jo.

'I told you you could come and ride her,' said Japhet, 'if you could get on.'

'We don't want favours,' the gipsy snarled. 'We're honest people whatever you might think. You won't get a better price anywhere else.'

Nothing would convince him. Their mother offered him a cup of tea, but he wouldn't even have that, nor would he let Danny accept a biscuit. He dragged the boy off roughly, and went away grumbling and muttering about dogs in the manger, and some people thinking they were better than other people – and after he'd looked after Jo for a week too.

'– Which he didn't,' said Japhet, 'because he was picking strawberries.'

The episode left them all a little downcast and uneasy; they weren't used to making enemies, and Louisa felt somehow, some time, that gipsy would try to get his own back. He had a very nasty look in his eye; she hoped she wouldn't ever meet him on the common. Her mother and father shrugged the whole thing off, and said he was just stupid, and not to worry. They were more concerned to find out whether the Society would let them keep Jo after all.

But Louisa felt in her bones that they hadn't seen the last of that gipsy. And what she felt in her bones was generally right.

Chapter Eight

On Sunday morning, to their great surprise, Danny turned up. They were still having breakfast when he appeared at the back door, looking as if he had slept in his clothes. But his grimy face was bright with expectancy.

'Come for me ride,' he said. 'You promised.'

'Does your father know?' their mother asked. Danny looked very small to be out alone.

'No,' he grinned. 'He'd belt me if he did.'

'Then hadn't you better go back?'

'It's all right, 'e don't get up, Sundays. Can I 'ave a go of 'er now?'

'Have you had breakfast?' asked Japhet with his mouth full of toast.

'Chips,' nodded Danny. There was grease round his mouth.

'Come on, then,' said Japhet, 'but I doubt if you'll be able to get near her.'

He was wrong. There was something about Danny that no pony could resist. As soon as he got into the field, Jo ambled towards him and stood still, nuzzling him, as if she were simply waiting to be ridden. Such a thing had never happened before. They all stared in astonishment as Danny and Jo held a short conversation; Jo's eyes didn't roll at all.

'Got a box or sunthin'?' asked Danny. 'She's a bit 'igh.'

Japhet fetched one of the kitchen chairs. When Jo saw him coming with it, her nearest eye did begin to roll – but Danny only patted her neck and talked to her, and she was as quiet as before. Then he stood on the chair, heaved himself over her back – and was off.

It was an amazing sight. Danny's short trousered legs stuck out almost straight on each side of Jo's broad back; at first he held on to her mane, but after a few minutes he let go, and gave such a performance as they had never seen outside a circus. Up and down, backwards and forwards and sideways he made Jo go – he even squirmed round and rode facing the wrong way. And to round it off, he knelt up, and then with one quick scramble was on his feet – and arrived back at the barbed wire standing astride in triumph, his face one big grimy grin, and Jo as steady as a rock.

'How did you learn to ride like that?' asked Japhet.

'Dunno.' He jumped neatly down.

'Can I try? Can I try?' said Rose, prancing about.

'But who taught you? Somebody must have,' said Louisa.

'Nobody. I just gets on and does it. We 'ad a pony once,' Danny explained, 'only Dad flogged 'er.'

'Do you mean he beat her?' Louisa was not surprised.

'No – flogged 'er. Took her to market. 'E wanted the money. She was black,' he added, 'littler'n this one. We called 'er Jet. I used to teach 'er tricks, like to lay down dead. She was gettin' on lovely. Then Dad flogged 'er.'

'Please let me try now,' begged Rose; but at the very

sight of anyone but Danny approaching, Jo rolled her eyes and stamped warningly; she would have nothing to do with them.

'That child certainly has got a way with horses,' said their mother, who had been watching from the kitchen window. 'But I do think he ought to be sent home before there's trouble.'

But sending Danny home was easier said than done. He was thoroughly enjoying himself.

When dinner-time came, he said that was all right, he could stay, he didn't have to go home. Louisa whispered to Japhet that perhaps he was afraid to – which Japhet could well believe, from what he had seen.

'Look here,' he said, taking Danny aside, 'would you like to come and live with us?' Danny stared blankly.

'I could ask our mother,' said Japhet, 'I'm sure it'd be all right.' This was what he always thought; unlike Louisa, he lived on hopes rather than plans.

'And 'ave our caravan in your field?' said Danny, brightening. 'Mum and Dad and Jim and –'

'I didn't mean that,' said Japhet hastily, 'Just you. We've got a spare bed. And you could ride every day, and teach us. After all, it's not very nice where you live, is it?'

'It's all right,' said Danny, looking obstinate.

'But I mean, do they really hit you?'

' 'Course – what about it?'

'Well, *we* wouldn't,' said Japhet. 'My father doesn't believe in it.' Danny looked at him as if he were either a liar or a lunatic.

'What's wrong with 'ittin, then? All boys 'it.'

'But I thought – I mean, wouldn't you rather live here, in a proper house?'

'No,' said Danny.

Japhet was puzzled. His good intentions didn't seem to be getting him very far. He had had the sudden inspiration of 'adopting' Danny – he had always wanted a younger brother, and to get Danny away from that awful family would surely be killing two birds with one stone. (Japhet didn't of course, know what 'adopting' meant; he thought you just said 'O.K.' and did it.)

But here was Danny staring at him quite stonily and not wanting to be adopted at all.

'I thought you liked it here.'

'It's all right.'

'Well, then –'

'I never said it wasn't.'

'But wouldn't you like to have an electric train to play with?'

'Not special.'

'– And people not hitting you all the time?'

'I can duck, can't I?' Japhet turned away; it was hopeless. He changed the subject.

'Want to see my treasures?' Danny was alert at once.

'Come on, I'll show you. A ceiling fell down, and we found these things hidden in the roof, there was an old man here, you see, and he might have been very rich – but it's a secret, specially the papers, because –'

He was cut short by the violent jangling of the old cow-bell that was kept on the corner of the kitchen mantelpiece. It was a real Swiss one, with a horn clapper.

'That means dinner,' said Japhet, vaguely realising

79

that it had rung several times before.

'I'll wait for you.' Danny climbed on to the roller and started to do a balancing trick.

'What about your own dinner?'

'Oh, Mum won't mind. As long as we keep out of the way.'

'I'll ask if you can have some of ours.'

'I'd rather 'ave another go on that pony.'

In the end, they had almost to force him to go home. Talk about hints, thought Louisa – he was unsquashable.

Their father took hold of his shoulders, turned him gently round, and propelled him down the path.

'And mind that main road!'

Danny didn't turn round; he was whistling to himself, and making soft 'pony noises' as he plodded slowly through the long grass.

'I hope you didn't go and tell him anything,' said Louisa to Japhet after dinner. 'You seemed to be doing a lot of talking out there.'

'Tell him what?'

'About You-Know-Who.'

'The Captain? No. No, I didn't.'

'– Or the things we found. Or the ceiling. Or the well.'

'No – well, that is, no. Anyway, why not?'

'Are you sure?' Louisa was suspicious.

'Yes,' said Japhet, feeling slightly shaken. Louisa did go on as if you were in a law court. 'Anyway,' he repeated, 'why are you so worried?'

'Because you never know,' said Louisa.

'*What* don't you?'

'It's that gipsy, really,' she explained. 'I've got a horrid feeling about him.'

'Well, Danny's all right,' said Japhet casually. 'He's too young to understand anything. Except ponies.'

'I'm not so sure,' said Louisa. 'Gipsies are always older than they look.' And with these wise words she left Japhet to go and get those papers; she intended to have a thorough examination of them that afternoon.

Japhet had a twinge of conscience, but it didn't last long; after all, he hadn't told Danny anything worth remembering; and Danny hadn't seemed very specially interested. He gave Louisa the sealed bundle; she spread them out on a bed to read.

All was quiet and safe: the curtains were drawn against the hot sun, making the bedroom greenish-cool, like a secret tank. Outside, their mother was sunbathing and their father cutting the grass, that would take them all afternoon. Not a sound but the buzz of a few flies, a distant plane, the lawnmower – and Rose's dolls singing 'Good King Wenceslas', one at a time, in another bedroom. (It was the nearest thing to a hymn that Rose knew right through, and the dolls were in church.)

Louisa realised almost at once what the papers were. It was like being given a great familiar pat on the back by someone you recognised as soon as you turned round. Of course – Noah Fogwill's cuttings about wills! Already she was beginning to feel she knew the old man; she could see his large brown hand holding the scissors and carefully snipping out the piece every day – in case, just in case. . . . But what had he hoped? If his uncle's name didn't appear in any of these, why cut them out?

'Well?' asked Japhet. 'What are they?'

'Wills. Advertisements for people who might be missing heirs –'

'What did I tell you, what did I say? Yippee, hooray, we've got it!' Japhet glowed and beamed and hopped hysterically about.

'Got what?' said Louisa.

'Well, what it's all about. You were the one who said, you should know.'

'We know,' said Louisa slowly and clearly, 'that the Captain used to cut out wills. We knew that before. And here they are. But where d'you think that gets us? Absolutely nowhere. Unless,' she reflected, 'you could say it proves the Gillingses were telling the truth. But I never thought they weren't, anyway.'

'But if all these are no good, why didn't he throw them away?'

'Just what I was thinking.'

'They *must* be some good. One of them must. Perhaps he was short-sighted; or perhaps he couldn't read properly. And he was waiting for somebody to come and go through them with him, and they never came –'

'A sea-captain would be able to read,' said Louisa, 'even in those days.' Still, there might be something in the short-sighted idea, otherwise, all this hoarding of papers seemed quite pointless. Unless he really was mad. . . .

'I haven't read through them all yet,' she said. 'Perhaps there was something he missed.'

Just then, a slight breeze blew the curtains inwards, and some of the papers fluttered to the floor.

'Hey!' Japhet paused on his hands and knees. 'What

82

name did you say?'

'Fogwill. I suppose it's F, O, G –'

'It couldn't be FROGWELL, could it?' said Japhet.

'Where?' Louisa was down on the floor with him. The advertisement seemed to rise up and hit her in the eye.

'RE HORATIO GEORGE FROGWELL, DE-CEASED,' she read, '– Persons having a claim against or an interest in the Estate of Horatio George Frogwell, of Wagga Wagga, New South Wales –'

'Wagga Wagga!' Japhet rolled over, shrieking with laughter.

'What's so funny?' said Louisa. 'Listen, for goodness sake –' and she read the rest of the advertisement, which said that Horatio George had died on the 1st April, 1949, and anyone who had a claim on his estate should send it in writing to a firm of London lawyers called Blogg, Banks and Heppelwhite, in Cannon Street.

'It must be him, it must be!' said Japhet.

'Well, it might,' Louisa allowed, trying to sound cautious, though she really felt wildly excited. It was more than she had dared to hope. There remained the puzzle – why was the advertisement still with all the rest; why had Noah kept all the others; why hadn't he taken this one and made his claim?

'I'm going round to see the Gillingses,' Louisa announced, and sprang to action.

'Where are you going?' asked Rose, whose dolls would, of course, have just finished their service at that moment.

So the Gillings's Sunday nap was disturbed by three panting children, led by Louisa, who burst straight out with 'Was it Fogwill or Frogwell, and when did he actually disappear, and was he blind or anything, or short-sighted?'

Mr and Mrs Gillings blinked and took some time to get over this invasion.

'Steady on now, steady on,' said Mr Gillings, 'you'd better all 'ave drinks, you look properly puffed.' And Mrs Gillings insisted on pottering about getting lemonade, while Mr Gillings asked them how their Dad was keeping, and other uninteresting questions.

'You mean the Captain,' he said at last. 'Well, I reckon it might've been Frogwell, I'm not all that good on names. And 'e never 'ad no letters, not that I know of. 'E was a lone sort of bird, if you know what I mean.'

'But he could read and write?' persisted Louisa.

'Oh he could, yes. Until 'e went blind, that is.'

'*Blind*?' She jumped as if she had heard a shot.

'Well, near enough – didn't I tell you? It was towards the end 'is sight began to go –'

'Why, 'e once put salt in 'is tea,' began Mrs Gillings – 'Wouldn't let you do anything for 'im, though, 'e was too proud.'

'Thank you, thank you!' said Louisa. 'It's just what we wanted to know!'

And they left the Gillingses shaking their heads in astonishment.

'Not only homeless but *blind*,' said Louisa on the way home. 'That just about finishes it! My goodness, if I ever met that Mr Glover – he ought to be put in prison!'

'Have you ever tried salt in tea?' said Rose.

'We must find him now, we simply must,' said Louisa, striding on ahead. 'He probably just went on cutting out those pieces without being able to read them properly, only he'd know where they came in the paper, he'd been doing it for so long; and he was too proud to ask anyone to help – oh, it's awful!'

'Suppose the money had been claimed by the wrong person –' began Japhet.

'It couldn't be, the lawyers wouldn't let it.'

'What would happen to it, then?'

'I don't know – oh do come *on*, Rose!'

'Well, they do put it in coffee,' said Rose, trotting along behind.

'Honestly,' Japhet protested, 'she is dim!'

'Oh well,' said Louisa, being tolerant, 'she's only young.'

But brothers and sisters can misjudge each other; and even the youngest may do something unexpected. Louisa had perhaps forgotten that Rose had a mind of her own.

Chapter Nine

'I shall take it to a museum,' said Japhet.

'What for?' Derek said.

They were back at school; the skull, wrapped in two paper bags, lay in Japhet's desk. He had asked Miss Gibbon, his teacher, what it was, and she had been most unhelpful.

Derek didn't mind the stink, but he wasn't much interested in the skull itself. After all, he lived for pigs.

But Japhet had once read a piece in the local paper about their digging up bones and bits of old pots on the hills. And in spite of Louisa, he still thought this might be a Roman dog – in which case, the museum would surely pay for it – perhaps pounds. Anyway, the thought was worth a threepenny bus ride.

He put his paper bag down on the table inside the door. A girl with glasses was selling postcards there – or would have been, if there had been anyone to buy them. The place was empty. But Japhet wasn't showing any skulls to her; she'd probably behave like Miss Gibbon.

'Can I see the keeper?' he asked.

'You mean the curator? I'll see if he's in. What's your name, please?' He told her. Was it about anything special? she asked doubtfully – and stupidly, he thought. You wouldn't go seeing keepers of museums for nothing.

'I'll tell him when I see him,' he said, standing his ground. 'It may be important.' The girl glanced sharply at the paper bag and went away.

– Probably thought something was going to jump out, Japhet said to himself; pity he hadn't brought one of those toads from under the lavender bushes. Standing among all the glass cases, with their faded labels, he felt they needed something alive in here, even a toad.

It was a drab little museum, full of rows and rows of rusty bits of iron; some of the labels had got turned upside down or fallen off, and no-one had bothered. Japhet thought how if he had a museum, he would fill it with swords and pistols and painted figureheads off ships; he would have flags, and some armour, and a model of a sputnik, and plenty of skeletons. – And perhaps some wax figures of cave-men trying to light a fire, or skinning an animal, with a green lamp to make it look ghastly. And plenty of sticky blood, as he had once seen in the Chamber of Horrors. But he'd have music played on records all the time, to cheer people up, as in Woolworth's. Some slot-machines for chocolate, and a target where people could try out the guns or bows and arrows for sixpence a time. . . .

Japhet was quite carried away with the colour and noise of his dream-museum when he heard a dry voice at his shoulder.

'Yes? What can I do for you?'

The voice reminded Japhet that it was a hot afternoon, that all the windows were shut, and that his paper bag definitely smelt. (Added to which, he should have been home for tea; but that could be dealt with later.)

The man looked at the bag and drew back. Japhet noticed that his appearance was as dusty as his museum; grey clothes, streaky grey hair, rimless spectacles and a face like the pale yellow blotting-paper they were given at school. But his expression was not unkind; simply tired.

'It's a skull,' he said when Japhet opened the bag.

'I know. I just wondered what of.'

'A dog, I should think. Why have you brought it here? What do you want me to do with it?' The man sounded weary, as if he were almost at the end of his tether already, and in no mood for seeing skulls.

'I thought it might be an ancient dog, that's all,' said Japhet.

'It smells ancient enough.'

'I mean Roman or Ancient British or something.'

'Egyptian, perhaps?' said the man with a very faint smile.

'I thought they went in for cats.'

'Look here, I think you'd better take it away, you know, and give it a decent burial.'

'Couldn't you just say roughly the date?'

'I'm afraid I'm not a vet.'

'– Not even the century?' said Japhet reproachfully. 'I thought you'd be sure to know that. I thought that's what musuems were for.'

'If it had been a few thousand years old,' said the man, 'I might have helped.' His voice had a distant and melancholy sound, as if he really wished he lived in the past, and was in fact half there. 'All I can say about this,' he went on, 'is Recent.'

'Recent dog,' Japhet murmured, putting it thoughtfully back into the paper bag. The girl winced as he touched it. 'I suppose that's not worth much, then. Still, I think I'll keep it; somebody might recognise him.'

'You must do as you think best,' said the man, holding a handkerchief to his nose. And then, as Japhet looked rather crestfallen, 'thank you for letting us have the opportunity of seeing the specimen. Good afternoon.' And he faded back to wherever he had come from; probably some dusty place full of tusks and dried-up inkwells, Japhet imagined.

'I'm sorry to have bothered you, Mr Glover,' called the girl as he went.

Japhet stood stock-still. *Glover*! Wasn't that the name of the man Louisa was so angry about? For a moment he thought of pursuing him into his den and challenging him; then he decided no; that wasn't the sort of thing real detectives did. They turned up their raincoat collars and drove away in fast cars to find more clues.

Japhet hadn't a raincoat or a fast car, so he turned up his blazer and mooched off to the bus, giving very penetrating sidelong glances at passers-by; those who noticed wondered uneasily if they had buttons undone or smuts on their noses.

'It's quite a common name,' said Louisa – but decided, all the same, to write to Mr Glover of the museum and ask him if he knew anything about N. Fogwill or Frogwell. If he didn't, it could do no harm; if he did, surely his conscience would stir him enough to provide some clue, however vague? Not for Louisa the methods of TV sleuths; she got her fountain pen out straight away.

'P.S.,' she ended, 'we think he wore about size twelve boots, at *least*.'

Now all she had to do was to wait for the post. – All, that is, until next Saturday, when she would be taking the first great step of her own.

That night the weather broke. It had been really too hot for days now, still and sticky, so that even the cold tap ran warm, and it was no good buying choc ices unless you ate them at once.

By tea-time people were talking of thunder; and when their father came home he found his salad all over the draining-board, half-washed, while their mother frantically tore clothes off the line outside, her hair dripping into her eyes and her face lashed with the wet of the sudden storm.

But what was much worse, it put the television out of order.

'And right in the middle of part two!' protested Japhet in a frenzy. 'It's not fair! I missed half 'The Blanco Kid' last week, and now *this*!'

In vain their father turned and twiddled; the set was dead.

'Perhaps the aerial's been struck,' he said, 'we'll have to get old Cuthbertson to come and have a look.'

'It's what's known as an Act of God,' said Louisa calmly. She didn't care for 'The Blanco Kid' herself.

Japhet said that still didn't make it fair; his freckles were puckered with disappointment, his hair stood on end; his voice squeaked; he was just a pink ball of indignation. Louisa couldn't help laughing – whereupon he stamped upstairs, and five minutes later was re-laying his electric train lines as if he hadn't a care in the world: in fact he sang 'Tea for Two' so loudly that Rose called out from her bed to say would he please not set up such a roar, she couldn't hear the thunder. Louisa and her parents marvelled at such a change of mood; but then, Japhet was like that.

Next day Mr Cuthbertson from the electric shop took away their old set and lent them a new one while the job was being done. A beauty, one of the latest models. Japhet looked at it with great approval, and spent many happy hours in front of it that week, eating the dough-nut he often bought on the way home from school, and getting sugar between his toes. (It came out if you combed the carpet with them.)

'Now where are those papers?' Louisa demanded on Friday evening. Tomorrow was her great day.

Already she had laid out her red and white striped dress for going to London tomorrow – together with hairband, purse, clean socks and plastic mackintosh. She always looked ahead.

'Oh, all right,' And Japhet tore himself away from the margarine advertisement and went out into the garden.

'What on earth –' began Louisa '– I thought you had them in a drawer?'

'I thought of somewhere better,' said Japhet, and started to lift the wooden pieces off the top of the well: of course the cement men hadn't come yet.

'You don't mean to say –'

'I'll get the ladder,' said Japhet. 'You know what the

man said, it's not deep. If anybody comes, just sit on it and cover it up.' He dashed off to the shed.

Louisa peered down into the well. 'Whatever did you want to go and put them in there for?' she said as Japhet dragged the ladder across the grass.

'Won't take a minute,' said Japhet. 'I wanted to hide them properly. I mean, it's no fun unless you do.' He was manipulating the ladder to get it over the edge of the well.

'Really, your idea of fun,' said Louisa.

But Japhet was too busy to answer: the ladder tilted, slid down the side, and then – splash!

They both stood astounded.

'I thought it was dry!' said Japhet.

'It was! – Oh you silly stupid ass,' burst out Louisa, 'it must have filled up with all that rain we had, that storm the other day – and *now* look what you've done! Gone and lost them!'

'They'd float,' said Japhet, 'wouldn't they?'

'I shouldn't think so, a bundle like that. Really, you are the limit! Why on earth couldn't you have left them where they were?'

'I thought it'd be more exciting,' said Japhet miserably. '– Well, what about hollow trees?' he demanded, turning on Louisa.

'What about them?'

'People hide things in them, don't they? And dungeons and places like that? Anyway, how was I to know it was going to rain?'

'They always say it after the news,' said Louisa. 'Besides, it's got to rain some time. Oh, I wish I'd kept the beastly papers myself –'

'I'm going down to see if they're there,' said Japhet; and before Louisa could stop him, he was half-way down the ladder. Guarding the open top of the well, she hoped and prayed her mother wouldn't come while Japhet was down there. But luckily she was busy cutting Rose's fringe; they could hear distant squawks of protest at the cold scissors.

'Good thing I hadn't got any shoes on,' said Japhet, coming up. His feet were black with slime; in his hand was a dripping, pulpy lump that had once been paper.

'Well, I should have thought you'd have copied it out, anyway,' he grumbled as Louisa gazed at the object with horror. 'Can't you remember it?'

'Why on earth should I? I don't go about remembering lawyers' addresses,' she snapped. '*Now* what am I to do?'

'But you don't know if the Captain's alive, yet. You might find he's dead.' At the moment, Japhet thought this would save a lot of trouble. '– Then there wouldn't be any point in going to the lawyers, anyway.'

'Oh well, I suppose I might not have had time to-morrow,' Louisa admitted. 'It may be as much as I can do to get away to go to Somerset House.' That last sentence sounded very old and experienced, and made her feel better. 'Anyway,' she added, 'you'd better put that soggy thing at the back of the airing-cupboard; it might dry out, then we should be able to read it again.'

But Japhet had a better idea.

Chapter Ten

Louisa stood under the great stone entrance arch of Somerset House. In the sunlight ahead lay the courtyard, partly cobbled, stretching away beyond the rows of cars to the symmetrical and serious buildings on the other side. In the foreground was a bronze statue of a naked man with a long beard and a large wreath, sitting with his back to a huge horn of plenty, and tipping something out of a pot. He pointed downwards to where it would have tipped if there had been anything in it. Above him stood a lady with a lion and a bit of a ship; these were dark against the fawnish expanse of courtyard and the glitter of car roofs. On her left, inside the deep porch, a notice saying 'Search Room Open to the Public'. On her right, Georgia, beginning a fit of the giggles.

'You're not really going in – oh honestly, you can't!'

That decided it. Louisa pulled herself together and marched to the door by the notice-board.

'You needn't come,' she said to Georgia.

'Whatever will you say? What will you ask? Oh, I shall burst!' giggled Georgia, 'You know I always do!'

'Well, don't,' said Louisa.

They went in.

Louisa clutched the cord of the bag that contained, among other things, a notebook and a newly-sharpened pencil. It was her beach-bag really, blue and white striped plastic. She wished she had something more official and studious-looking – but having got so far, she wasn't going to be put off by details; not even by Georgia.

The whole outing was a great stroke of luck. Georgia's parents had invited her to come up to town with them for the day; they were taking the girls out to lunch and tea and to a film.

'It's really a delayed birthday present,' Georgia explained, 'because on my actual birthday I had mumps. Do come!'

Of course, Louisa was only too glad. The one problem was, how to get away from them for a time, in order to do what she wanted. But this turned out to be easier than she expected. First she had to confide in Georgia – this she did with some qualms, because nice though Georgia was, she was a bit scatty, and might not understand that this was serious.

But Louisa need not have worried at all. Georgia thought it was a wonderful idea that they should go off together; she simply said to her parents in the train 'I say, will it be all right if Louisa and I muck about by ourselves for an hour this morning?' And that was that: no questions, no wondering whether it would be wise – just 'Oh, very well, darling; we'll meet for lunch in the Corner House. The one in the Strand where we always go with Auntie Mabel. Be by the sausages at one o'clock.'

As simple as that. You could see why Georgia was so happy-go-lucky; her parents didn't worry about her at all.

'Of course it works both ways,' Georgia remarked in a dry tone that was new to Louisa, '– she never even

95

bothered to come to the school play, she was out playing bridge. Still, I didn't really mind.'

Louisa decided that she'd rather have her own mother, in spite of everything. Even if she was apt to be late, she did turn up; she might be forgetful, but she was always interested; and although she was bad at sewing, she'd turn the house upside down for a helpful safety pin. . . .

They went into the entrance hall where there were two glass cases and a peculiar smell. The glass cases contained the birth certificates of William Wordsworth and some other people they had never heard of; the smell, Louisa thought, must be of old books and some special furniture polish.

'Come on,' she said, and led the way into another room, which to her surprise was almost exactly like a post office. A long counter with a metal grille; people filling in forms on ledges; other people going up to the men behind the counter just as if they were sending telegrams or taking out savings.

'Yes, Miss? Birth Certificates, is it?' said a kindly-looking man in a dark uniform. 'You fill up your Search form, give it in over there. Is it for a passport?'

'Well,' said Louisa slowly, trying not to look taken aback, 'as a matter of fact, no.' She saw, over one section of the counter, a notice saying 'Full Birth Certificates, 3/9.'

'Do I have to have a certificate?' she asked. 'All I wanted to do was look.'

'Ah well, in that case, just fill up a form for permission to go into the Search Room,' he said. And he gave Louisa a piece of pale yellow paper with columns for particulars.

She took it to one of the ledges, and stared at it in some dismay.

'It says "Date of birth",' she whispered to Georgia, 'how on earth am I to know when the Captain was born?'

Georgia craned over her shoulder. 'Look, though, underneath – something about "If the date of birth is unknown" –'

'– "State here the years you wish to search". But I haven't the faintest idea!' gasped Louisa. 'I thought you just went and looked up the name, not the date!'

'Can I help you, Miss?' The man in uniform smiled.

'Well, yes. I mean, no. I mean, thank you – but actually it's more whether somebody's dead that we wanted to find out. We know he was *born*.' The man took this calmly.

'Ah, you want Death Certificates. That's the other side of the archway. Straight across, you'll see the notice-board. Tell them you want a Death Certificate.'

'All right,' said Louisa, 'thank you very much.' Georgia followed her out.

'But you don't,' she whispered, '– do you? I thought –'

'Ssh! We might *have* to get one, I suppose: now for goodness sake don't giggle in there; remember it's deaths!'

They crossed the stone paving outside, and went into an entrance hall almost exactly like the first, except that here the oblong papers displayed in the glass cases were not about births. Louisa examined them.

Georgia brought out a bag of Turkish Delight.

'Not in here,' Louisa said, 'not where it says Deaths!'

'Anybody'd think it was a cemetery,' objected Georgia as they went in.

It was not quite so much like a post office; there was only a small counter barred off in one corner; some dark polished tables; and up above, a narrow gallery that ran round the room and held row upon row of enormous red books. On the wall was a notice saying you must pay 1/6 for searching.

'That allows for five years,' said Louisa, studying it.

'What, five years in here?'

'No, silly ass, five years of books. I suppose that means three shillings for ten years, and so on.'

'Six choc ices or half a riding lesson,' said Georgia. 'It's not worth it.'

But Louisa had gone up to the desk.

'Please,' she said, 'I'm looking for a man called Fogwill or Frogwell, the initial's N for Noah, here's one and six and can my friend come too?'

'D'you know what month and year he died?' asked the man behind the grille.

'I don't know that he *is* dead,' said Louisa. The man looked surprised. 'As far as I know he's still alive.'

The man scratched his head. 'Sounds to me as if you want the police.' he said. 'Lists of Missing Persons.'

'But can't I just look up the Frogwells?'

'Not unless you can suggest a rough date, Miss. You see all we've got up there –', waving his hand towards the gallery – 'it'd take you a lifetime!'

'We've got an hour,' said Louisa. She looked up to where people were creaking and rustling about among huge tomes. They all looked as if they knew exactly what they wanted; none of them, she felt sure, was uncertain whether anybody was dead or alive. She began to feel rather shaken, but she stuck to her point.

'If I can't look under 'Fs',' she said, 'I'd better try the last five years. Then if he's not down as dead in those, that'll have to be that. He was last seen about five years ago; he was alive then.'

'That's something,' said the man so seriously that she knew he was on the point of laughing at her. But never mind; she filled in the form and was shown, with Georgia, up a narrow staircase into the gallery.

There, another man led them to some shelves where the great red books had Louisa's suggested dates stamped on their backs in gold.

'Here you are, Miss,' said the second man, 'it's all yours!'

Louisa stood thunderstruck.

A volume for every year would have been bad enough – but there was one for every month!

'Sixty books!' groaned Georgia, and got out her Turkish Delight in desperation.

'Well, we'd better start,' said Louisa when she had recovered from the first shock. 'I'll take January, you take February, and we'll go on like that.'

They hauled out the first two tomes. For the next three-quarters of an hour they worked steadily through the first two and a half years; there were Fogwills and a few Frogwells, but no Noah.

'Thank goodness he's got an unusual name,' panted Louisa, changing her volume for the fifteenth time.

'There's somebody here called Egbert!' said Georgia – 'Egbert Fogwill!' – and spluttered Turkish Delight sugar all over the page.

'Don't waste time,' Louisa told her, 'and blow that off.'

Georgia blew the white powder into the crevice between the pages, hastily closed the book and put it back.

'It's getting late,' she said, 'if we're not there my mother'll probably go in without us, and make my poor father wait, and he hates that.'

'But there's another two and a half years to do!' protested Louisa.

'Perhaps that man would help us,' said Georgia, 'if we gave him a tip.' She glanced at the uniformed official.

'No,' said Louisa firmly after a moment's thought. 'I'm going on until I've finished. You go to lunch, and tell your mother I got held up.'

'What by?'

'Just held up, that's all. That's what my father always says.'

'Oh, all right,' said Georgia. 'You'd better take the last bit of this stuff, in case you starve.'

And she gave Louisa the crumpled paper bag.

But once you had got into the way of it, finding the names was quicker. And left to herself, without Georgia making funny remarks, Louisa concentrated and made steady progress. By August of the fifth year, she had still found no Captain Noah; by November she was thinking about sausages and chips; as she thankfully heaved December back into its place she had a definite vision of ice cream with chocolate sauce.

'Find what you wanted, Miss?' asked the man in uniform. 'You know how to fill in the particulars, do you?'

'Thank you, I think I would if there were any,' said

Louisa politely. 'But my person seems to be alive.'

'Oh,' said the man, astonished.

'Anyway, he's not here.'

'Ah well, they're all here, you know. Everyone born in Great Britain since 1837. No matter where death took place; Honolulu, Tibet, Iceland –'

But Louisa only wanted her lunch. So she thanked him and said goodbye and hurried out into the Strand. From a bus, she gazed at the passing crowds, and although it was quite ridiculous, she couldn't get it out of her head that somewhere the Captain might be there, walking about. . . .

At any rate, she was sure he was alive.

Chapter Eleven

'Go and get some matches,' Japhet told Rose. '– And if they say "What for?" just say "Nothing".'

'That's no good,' said Rose, 'they'll only go on and on, like they did about my nature notebook.'

'Like who did?'

'Miss Bleakie.' There had been a fuss about that Nature notebook that Rose would not forget for a long time. Miss Bleakie had not seen the connection between ponies and nature at all.

But Japhet waved the whole matter aside.

'Oh, school!' he said scornfully. 'That's different. Besides, it's Saturday,' he added, as if that made anything possible. Derek was there, and it would have looked so feeble to have to give reasons for wanting just a box of matches.

Rose left them sitting by the big oak tree in the wood.

When she came back, they were looking at Derek's air-gun, which his mother had told him not to bring.

'I could get a rabbit from here,' he said, pointing it towards the field.

'How horrible,' said Rose, 'a poor rabbit!'

'It's all right, it's not loaded.'

'Japhet's not even allowed to play with matches.'

'Well, nor are you!' Japhet was angry; he hated to be made to look silly in front of Derek.

'Anyway,' Rose persisted, '*I* wouldn't go burning great holes in cushions!'

'Oh yes you would.'

'Not on the patterned side.'

'Oh shut up, that was donkeys years ago.'

'They were the best cushions,' Rose persisted. 'I don't see why you had to make ordinary Indians use the best cushions.'

'Well, we're not playing Indians now,' said Japhet, 'and there are no cushions here. Make a draught, somebody!'

He was on his knees, trying to light a fire in the wood. Derek leaned his gun against a tree and started to flap his jacket at the growing nest of smoke. Ash flew up into their eyes; the fire went out.

'Give us the matches,' said Derek.

But for all his carrying on as though he were born and bred to light fires in woods, he couldn't make it go either.

'Timber's damp,' he said, kicking it. 'Must be.'

'What about two bricks,' suggested Japhet, 'with the box on top, and the fire underneath? There'd be a proper current of air then.'

He picked up a tin biscuit box, and for the fourth time looked inside to make sure the damp papers were there. Yes; all they needed was cooking. Japhet had imagined the tin lying in the red embers; he would only have to turn it over a few times; after about half an hour, he judged the papers inside would be as safe and crisp as ever.

But when they had finished the second box of matches, even Japhet decided it would have to be the airing cupboard after all. A pity.

They kicked the ashes apart, picked up the tin and the gun and went back to the house.

'Hey!' said Japhet suddenly, 'I'd almost forgotten: it's "The Black Riders!" Here, Rose, you put this in the cupboard. . . .' And Rose was left clasping the biscuit tin, while the boys dashed headlong into the sitting-room and threw themselves on the floor in front of TV.

'It's not fair,' she said to her mother, 'Japhet having Derek to tea *again*. Why can't I have somebody? And I don't mean Sarah Carter,' she added, 'because she's my worst friend.'

'I thought you said she was your best?'

'That was last week.'

'All the same,' her mother began – but she never finished the sentence.

A sharp bang: a smash of glass. They both jumped like rabbits.

'What on earth was that?' Rose's mother dashed into the sitting-room, to find Derek bending over the TV, and Japhet standing a few feet away with a scarlet face – and a gun!

'I couldn't help it,' he began, 'he said it wasn't loaded –'

'Whatever have you done?'

'It's dead all right,' said Derek, standing back. 'Gone right through. Must have hit a valve.'

In the centre of Mr Cuthbertson's magnificent set there was a splintered hole; bits of glass glittered on the carpet.

'Japhet! What *have* you done?'

'Shot the telly,' said Derek, 'that's all.'

'*All!*'

'I tell you, I didn't think it was loaded,' protested Japhet frantically. 'I only pointed it in fun, pretending we were hidden in an ambush, and when the Black Riders came by – well, I couldn't *help* it!' he shouted in desperation. 'He *said* it wasn't loaded!'

'Didn't think it was,' mumbled Derek, 'Dad must have had it out last night.'

'Look here, you'd better take your gun and go home,' said Japhet's mother.

'But what will Mr Cuthbertson say?' Rose asked. 'Now he'll have to mend this one too!'

'It may not be able to be mended,' their mother said grimly. 'And goodness knows what we shall do then; your father certainly can't afford to pay for it. Really, Japhet, you must be mad!'

Japhet stood dumb and miserable and enraged. He felt bitterly that it was all Derek's fault. The fact that he was the one who had fired was only bad luck: just because he happened to be enjoying the programme more.

'How much do they cost?' asked Rose. 'More than ten shillings?'

'Don't be an idiot!' Japhet let loose his fury on her, for want of a better target. His mother had gone to see Derek and his gun safely off the premises.

'Well I don't shoot things, anyway,' retorted Rose.

'You'd probably miss if you did, fatty.'

'I wouldn't, and I'm not!' Rose's eyes filled with tears. She would rather be called anything but this. It was the one certain spark for a real quarrel. But their mother pounced in and separated them. Japhet was sent up to his bedroom, while Rose moped around at a loose end, wishing she had asked Sarah Carter to tea after all. It had not been a very nice Saturday.

Their father, coming back as usual from his cricket, said the business of the TV set was really the very last straw. The absolutely final straw. The end.

But he spoke too soon.

Chapter Twelve

Louisa didn't hear the telephone. She was sleeping heavily, after her day in London. Vaguely, perhaps in a dream, she registered an unusual stir about the house; some thumps, some footsteps, and opening and shutting of doors.

But what really woke her up was the fire engine. Clang, quick clang, repeat clang, urgent unmistakeable clang, down the road in front of the house; then the roar of engines, gears changing as it turned into their rutted drive; then shouts, tramping of feet.

'What's happened?' she said, wide awake at her bedroom door. Japhet rushed past, fastening up his boiler suit over his pyjamas.

'The wood's on fire!' he said. 'Come on!'

Louisa went to the window. There, across the field, a red glow lit up the sky. The air reeked of smoke. There were flames that silhouetted the trees in the foreground. The grass flickered gold, dark, gold, in patches near the edge of the wood. She could see figures running across the field.

In two minutes she was running too, having snatched her jeans and an old jersey from a bottom drawer; she didn't bother about shoes.

The fire brigade were dragging their hose across the field; some men bent over its brass joints; others ran on;

others were scurrying round the fire engine that stood giving a Christmassy glitter of red and gold in the dark by Jo's gate.

Over by the wood, Louisa found her parents, and, of all people, the dapper Mr Carter. It seemed that he and his wife had been driving home from a party when they saw the fire; he had stopped at his house to telephone, and had then come on to see if he could help.

Japhet was tagging along behind the firemen who led the way into the wood with the hose; his mother spotted him and called him back.

'A tree might fall!' she said.

'It's mostly small stuff,' Mr Carter pointed out, 'as long as it doesn't get that big oak.'

'– Or spread,' said their father. 'It's still pretty dry in there, even after all that rain. Thank heavens there's no wind.'

The hose was turned on; the smoke thickened and drove them back, choking. Louisa blinked against the smuts; a warm tear crawled down her cheek, though really she was far from crying, The high sparks, the flames against the black night sky, filled her with excitement. At the same time, the sensible side of her knew that the whole thing was really terrible; even if they did get the fire under control, what would the wood look like in the morning? Would it be razed to the ground, black and wet? Already she started to think about digging up some of those baby trees you sometimes saw in the hedges, to plant a new wood.

'How did it start, then?' She jumped. Out of the darkness, a small figure appeared at her elbow. ·

'Danny! Whatever are you doing here?'

'We saw the light in the sky, right from our place. I come over with Dad and Jim.'

'Where are they, then?' Louisa felt an immediate chill of uneasiness; she couldn't tell why.

'Oh, somewhere around,' said Danny casually. 'Where's Jo?'

'In the field, I suppose. D'you think she'll be frightened?'

'Might've took it into 'er 'ead to do a bolt. I'll 'ave a look.' And Danny darted away and disappeared into the smoke.

Louisa saw Jim, then, standing in the shadows by the men who were managing the hose. She thought she also saw — but couldn't be sure — a black figure slinking along the hedge on the further side of the field, going away from the fire and towards the house. But when she screwed up her eyes to look again, it had disappeared.

Then Jim turned and caught sight of her. He slouched over.

'Where's Danny?' he demanded.

'I don't know. Gone to look for Jo.'

'Your brother was after kidnappin' 'im,' Jim said in a nasty voice. ' 'E'd better look out. That's a crime, that is.'

'I don't know what you're talking about.'

'Oh no? My Dad was 'oppin' mad, I can tell you. Tryin' to get a little kid away from 'is 'ome. Bribin' 'im –'

'Look here,' said Louisa angrily, 'you'd better shut up.'

'You callin' me a liar?'

'I say,' said Japhet, coming across to them, 'did you

109

see that branch fall off the oak tree? If anybody'd been underneath –'

'Pity it wasn't you,' said Jim, and walked away.

'Whatever's the matter with *him*?' Japhet asked, amazed.

'He's mad,' said Louisa. 'I don't like him at all. I wish they hadn't come prying about here, it gives me a funny feeling.'

'Look, the fire's nearly out now. Hey, there's Danny! He's on Jo!'

'Don't make too much fuss of him, for goodness sake; they think we've been trying to kidnap him.'

But Japhet had already gone to greet Danny, who appeared, at first, as if he were borne aloft by the smoke, his rough fair hair picked out by the light of torches and lanterns, apparently sailing alone, until you saw Jo's ears and nose and plodding hooves below.

'She's all right,' he grinned. 'I got 'er steadied down.'

'Good thing you came,' said Japhet kindly, 'she might have gone mad.'

'Look, they're winding up the hose, it's all safe,' Louisa said.

'Get off there! Go on, get down!' Jim came up, furious. 'If Dad catches you larkin' about up 'ere again, 'e'll give you such a tannin' –'

'He wasn't doing any harm,' said Japhet, 'he's just saved our pony.'

'You keep your big gob shut!'

'Same to you!'

A breeze had cleared the smoke for a few seconds; Danny sat surveying the scene, like a king on a battle-field.

'Teachin' 'im to think we're scum!' stormed Jim.

'What's all this in aid of?' Japhet was really astonished.

'Givin' us a bad name – mind your tongue don't get blisters!'

Jim was edging up towards Japhet menacingly.

'Oh, get out of the way,' said Japhet.

'Get out yourself!'

That did it. Suddenly, to Louisa's horror, they were flying at each other, hitting out wildly, panting, scuffling, rolling about on the ground.

And Danny, who had jumped down off Jo, pranced excitedly around them shouting 'come on, Jim! 'It 'im, Jim! Let 'im 'ave it!' – and such like phrases of encouragement. Louisa stood appalled. 'Stop it! she shrieked. 'Go it, Jim!' squeaked Danny.

The ingratitude, thought Louisa – and then, just as Jim had seized a handful of Japhet's hair and Japhet was shoving his knee into Jim's stomach, up came Mr Carter.

'What's all this?' He dragged the boys apart.

They stood there, panting and silent. A trickle of blood ran from Jim's nose; it shone in the light of Mr Carter's big torch.

'Look, 'e's bleedin'!' said Danny. Jim wiped it with his sleeve.

' 'E's a dirty fighter!' he said. 'Look what 'e's done to me, then – wait till my Dad 'ears – 'e'll 'ave the law on you –'

'You'd better clear off,' said Mr Carter firmly.

'That's right, turn me out – 'e started it –'

' 'E did an' all, mister, 'e 'it my brother, right in the cake-'ole! I see 'im!' There was no doubt where Danny's feelings lay when it came to a crisis; Japhet stared at him, and suddenly realised what people meant when they said blood ran thicker than water.

'Clear off, the pair of you,' said Mr Carter,' – and you'd better come and report to your father,' he told Japhet.

Louisa realised that her parents must have gone back across the field to the fire engine. 'Oh don't tell him, please don't tell him,' she begged. 'Japhet's been in enough trouble already.'

Japhet looked at her gratefully; the blood business, sticking up for the family, worked both ways after all.

'Quick march,' said Mr Carter, and they plodded soberly towards the house. Not another word was said about the fight.

Their mother made cocoa and got out the biscuit tin and the cake tin and a bun-round that had been meant for Sunday's tea; by the time everyone had finished there was nothing left.

'What beats me,' said one of the firemen, dipping the last ginger nut into his cup, 'is how it started.' Japhet looked the other way. After all, he reasoned to himself, there hadn't actually been any bad damage done, and it was really jolly lucky to have been able to call the fire engine and have all that fun with only a few little trees being burnt. It was the sort of adventure that might happen only once in a lifetime. . . . Japhet soon began to feel he had really done the family a thoroughly good turn. As long as Rose didn't start blabbing about those matches. . . But for the time being, at any rate, Rose was safely out of the way. She had slept through the whole thing!

'Why didn't you wake me up?' she complained bitterly the next morning, 'It's not fair!'

But nobody took much notice of her; they were too busy hunting for their mother's engagement ring, which was missing from the saucer by the draining-board, where she always put it when she was washing up.

'Probably in one of your pockets,' said their father. 'Or upstairs. Sure to turn up.'

But he stopped being so casual when he went into his study later on that morning.

It had been ransacked.

Chapter Thirteen

'No,' said Louisa, 'I couldn't be *sure* it was him.'
Inwardly she was quite convinced that it was, in fact,
the gipsy who had slunk along the edge of the field;
but when you were confronted with a calm, pink-faced
police officer with a very sharp pencil and a notebook
you had to be careful.

'So far you've only noticed the ring missing?' the
detective said to their father.

'Yes; it's funny, I don't know what he thought he was
going to find in the study, but whatever it was, he was
unlucky.'

'Anything special he might have been looking for,
d'you think?'

'Can't imagine so. We don't have any hidden
treasures, worse luck!'

Japhet knew that his father meant this as a joke, but
he suddenly had a terrible pang: hadn't he said something to Danny? Might the boy have gone and repeated
it? — And got it all wrong, or put it so that the gipsy
might really have believed they had something valuable
hidden in the house? Five pound notes, or diamonds
or something? Japhet knew that Danny was not to be
trusted, except where Jo was concerned. Anything he
could do for his family, he would; their treatment of
him seemed to run off like water off a duck's back.

What if Danny had made that beastly father of his think Japhet's house was worth burgling? And what if the fire had given him just the opportunity he was waiting for?

Japhet began to feel very bad indeed. What with this *and* the TV set. . . .

And when the policeman had gone, there came the question Japhet most dreaded.

'What did you want those matches for yesterday?'

'Oh, that was to light a fire,' said Rose – and added, before Japhet could even pinch her, '– in the wood.'

So it all came out.

No more Derek to tea, no more matches, no more TV, no more going out to the wood at all without his parents or Louisa; he was to keep within sight until further notice. He was not to go into the garden shed, touch the well, talk to Danny. . . . Really, thought Japhet, life was hardly worth living.

Rose, who had a soft spot for anyone who was in trouble, took half a tube of fruit pastilles up to his bedroom, and said he could borrow her plastic whistle.

'What for?' said Japhet ungraciously.

'You could play "Good King Wenceslas" on it,' she said; '*that* can't do any harm.'

'And it isn't going to help us find the Captain, is it?' said Louisa dourly; she was beginning to feel it was hopeless to try to organise anything in this house. She had done her best – not much, perhaps, but even that little seemed to have led to trouble and more trouble.

'At any rate, you know he's not dead,' said Japhet.

Louisa was almost beginning to think it would be better if he were; as it was, she knew she would never be satisfied if she gave up the search now. The worse things got, the more important it seemed to hang on. The Captain had become part of her life. She felt she almost knew him and could see him fumbling for the sugar to put on his morning porridge. Perhaps he was in some Home where they grumbled at him for spilling it. Perhaps he was living by the sea, prodding his lonely way to the beach every day with a white stick, just to get a sniff of the ozone. And longing, always, for his old home . . . Louisa, sensible as she was, could make tears come into her eyes by such thoughts.

Rose gazed at her, now, with a stare of great concern. 'If we want to find him *very* much,' she said, 'why don't we just go out and look?'

'Don't be silly!' They turned on her with scorn. 'Where?' 'How?' 'What would be the use of that?' 'All right, go, then, if you can't think of anything better than that!' Louisa added in sheer exasperation.

'And what on earth Mr Cuthbertson's going to say about that television I don't know.' she went on. 'We shall just have no money left at all. Really, it's ghastly.' She was hunched on the floor, heavy with gloom. Japhet started to argue: neither of them noticed that Rose had gone quietly away.

It was tea-time; on Sunday there was generally fruit salad or a special cake.

'Where's Rose?' asked their mother.

They called; no reply.

'Probably in the wood,' said Japhet. They rang the cow-bell very loudly; Jo looked up, but there was no-one in the field or wood.

'That's funny. Perhaps she's gone to see Sarah Carter. I'd better ring up.'

But the Carters knew nothing.

'Perhaps she took Oats for a walk?'

But Oats was discovered fast asleep on one of the beds. Their father said again that it was time somebody kept an eye on that dog.

'She might have gone to Mrs Gillings,' Louisa suggested.

'Why? We went for the Sunday papers this morning.'

'She rather likes Mrs Gillings,' said Louisa lamely, 'that's all.'

'Well,' said their father, 'somebody had better go and see.'

'Not Japhet,' their mother said, 'he's done enough lately.'

So Louisa had to go. She thought it was very likely that she would find Rose sitting eating home-made coconut ice or something; it wasn't until she realised that the Gillings's cottage was empty that she even began to be worried.

By six o'clock, their parents were thoroughly alarmed. Even Japhet started to make suggestions, such as that Rose had gone to join the gipsies or been stolen by a tramp. . . .

'Don't be so silly,' said his mother angrily; 'Rose knows better than that.' But she was really angry because she was frightened.

By eight o'clock, when Rose should have been tucked up in bed, they had rung the police. Japhet and Louisa hung about the house with sober faces; Japhet said 'What if she's run away? There was a boy in the paper who ran away to France. He only got caught because he didn't know the French for bananas.'

'Couldn't he have done with an apple? Besides, why should Rose run away, nobody's even been cross with her today.' But Louisa's conscience was uneasy, and as if Japhet had read her thoughts, he suddenly said 'I say!' in an awe-stricken whisper – 'What if she really *has* gone to look for the Captain!'

'Surely she's not as batty as that!' But she was full of guilt and dismay. If Rose got an idea into her head. . . . And suppose something happened to her, it would be all Louisa's fault! The very thought so horrified her that she began to work out every possible argument against it. Rose must have more sense. She'd never try to do such a thing, and all alone.

But Louisa couldn't quite convince herself, and as for Japhet, he never had put any limit to the possible dimness of girls. . . .

But whereas he cheerfully thought Rose would be all right anyway, Louisa didn't.

'We ought at least to *ask* those gipsies,' she said to her mother.

'Yes, your father's gone round there.'

'They won't be very pleased to see him,' remarked Japhet.

'Whatever does that matter, now?' Their mother's voice shook.

'Perhaps he'll come back with her in a minute,' said Louisa, trying to sound soothing. 'Perhaps she's been playing with Danny. Shall I make you a cup of tea?'

'I couldn't swallow anything.'

But Louisa made it all the same; it was something to do. And she got out the aspirins and the remains of a bottle of tonic that said 'Fortifies the Nerves', and generally did her best.

But she was more frightened than surprised to see her father walk up the path alone.

'No,' he said, 'she' not there. Neither are the gipsies. They've cleared out, lock, stock and barrel.'

The bell rang. It was the same detective who had been in the morning about the burglary. But how unimportant a mere engagement ring seemed now!

He took notes as to the time of Rose's disappearance, her description, what she was wearing, whether she had any money, and various other things.

Their mother had discovered that Rose's pale blue cardigan had gone. There was one and sixpence in her money box.

'She *had* about two and fourpence altogether,' said Louisa, '– I know, because she asked me if it was enough to buy a paint box, and I said not a good one.'

'Well, don't worry too much,' said the detective, trying to be comforting. 'It's early yet. I expect we'll pick her up. Probably just went off exploring and lost her way – the kiddies will get up to these things.'

They cheered up a little – or pretended to. Japhet came the nearest to believing what the detective said, because he was always hopeful; but even he was far from happy.

'Don't you think we ought to tell them?' he said to Louisa when they were alone for a moment. 'I mean, about the Captain.'

'That's what I've been wondering. Though I don't

see what good it would do. Still, if she's not found soon, I think we'll have to. I wish to goodness we'd never heard of him! He's brought us nothing but bad luck.'

'It all sounds so daft,' said Japhet, 'when you come to think of it. Trying to find somebody you've never even seen. Just going out looking. Just anywhere, without a clue – she must be absolutely up the pole!'

'Don't say that!'

'Why not?'

'How would you feel if –'

'If what?' he muttered – though he suddenly knew what she was going to say.

'If anything really did happen to her!'

They decided to give themselves a time limit: if Rose were not found by ten o'clock, they would tell all about the Captain – for what that might be worth. Not much, they thought, but at least it might ease their consciences. . . .

It was just beginning to get dark. The nightingales had started up in the bushes on the corner of the common. Mr Gillings had once said they were a fair pest, keeping him awake.

But Louisa would have kept awake anyway, that night.

Across the landing, she heard Japhet snore. It was difficult not to think him heartless – but he couldn't help it, he always slept well, as soon as his head touched the pillow. Besides, he had been up nearly all the night before, with the fire. For that reason they had both been sent up early.

It was nearly half past nine.

Louisa lay watching the square of light at her window; it darkened, and there were no stars in it. She thought of Rose somewhere out there astray; she could hear the cars flashing back from a day at the sea; she could imagine how wet the grass would be with night dew. Would Rose have the sense to find a haystack or creep into a barn? Would she remember what she had been told about not speaking to strangers? If only the telephone would ring. If only Rose were safely home in bed. If only they had never heard of that wretched Captain. . . .

Louisa lay appalled by the utter lunacy of the whole affair. It was difficult to believe that she had ever cared so much about it, now that Rose was gone.

In half an hour Louisa would have to go down and tell her parents the whole ridiculous story. She felt the time creep by. Across the room, Rose's bed stood flat and neat in the twilight; downstairs, there was a new kind of quiet. The hall clock ticking – usually a friendly sound – now seemed sinister; the occasional rattle of teacups was not cheerful but sad, as if they were making tea in sheer despair. The very air in the bedroom seemed to be waiting with less and less hope as the last light went.

'And it's all my fault,' Louisa kept saying to herself. 'All my wretched fault!'

But at the same time, she was working out just how far you could get on a bus or train for about tenpence, child's fare. If you took a compass and drew a circle round the house, measuring this distance all round, at least you'd know what area Rose might be in. She

decided that at ten o'clock, if she did have to go downstairs, she would get out her geometry set and a map.

The clock ticked; Japhet snored; Louisa lay listening
to the nightingales, and wondered why she had ever
liked them.

Chapter Fourteen

'At home,' said Rose, 'I don't eat scrambled egg. But yours is nice.'

'I always put a bit of cheese with it,' said the fat lady with the gold tooth. '– And cook it very slowly. More cocoa, ducks? Warm you up.'

'No thank you. Is your tooth real?'

'What, real gold? Definitely. No National 'Ealth about that. Had it when I was a kid, after I fell off a tram. Give 'er the best, my Mum said, so he put gold.'

'I've never seen a tram.'

'Oh I used to love the trams. Long cheap rides we used to get, Saturdays –'

'Here, steady on,' broke in her husband, 'don't get started on that track, or we'll never be off. What about something to wrap her up in? It'll be coldish now.'

The lady went away to find an old jacket. Rose eyed the jam dish on the table.

'Is that strawberry?' she said.

The man nodded at her with a kindly twinkle, chewing.

This was how it had happened.

First, there was the red admiral butterfly on the common.

'Well, all right, I'll let you go,' Rose said to it. 'But Japhet wouldn't of.'

The butterfly fluttered out of sight. Rose sat thinking what a pity it was that you found things just when you weren't looking for them. She had spent hours by the lavender in the garden, trying to catch red admirals, and now here was one that had flown right on to her hand.

She had started off with the idea of walking along the road and asking whoever she met if they happened to have seen someone like the Captain. She knew the others would think this perfectly silly – but then, so was it silly to sit at home and do nothing. And she really believed she was lucky at finding things. And she thought how pleased they would be with her if she walked back leading the good old Captain, hand in hand and all smiles.

And in case none of these sound good enough reasons, remember that she was very bored that Sunday afternoon, and wanted something to do. And she didn't intend to go far. And perhaps that affair about the Nature notebook had a little to do with it, too: it had made her think that if you really wanted to find something, the safest way was to go and look and not say anything at all to anybody, or ask for any help.

It wasn't until she had been out for about an hour (ten minutes, *she* thought), that she realised that she had lost her way. She had taken a side turning that said 'To Winterfold Farm', because she liked the name; this lane led straight through a farmyard, where she was scared to go, in case someone came out and shouted at her. So then she climbed a gate into a field where there were wild poppies; she picked some of these, although she knew they really needed to be put in water straight away. In the field there was a scarecrow. She went and had a good look at that, because she and Japhet had tried to make one for the vegetable garden, and he hadn't worked. Birds just came and sat on him, and made white messes all over Japhet's old raincoat; their mother was cross, and said she had been saving that for Rose for next year. But the scarecrow in the field wasn't a particularly good one either; he didn't even have a face, or scarf; Rose thought any bird would see through that.

After crossing the field, she came to a wood where there were huge red fungi on the bottom of the trees; she knew she mustn't touch them in case she got poison on her fingers. But she found a broken bird's egg on the ground, and saw two squirrels. She always hoped she'd find a squirrel with a hurt paw, or some small thing the matter with it, so that she could take it home and nurse it and keep it for a pet. But these squirrels were clearly quite all right.

After the wood came another field, with cows. She spent some time stroking the tufty forehead of a specially clean-looking one.

Then she came out on to a road she didn't recognise. She had no idea of the direction to take, but there was some honeysuckle along the hedge on the right, so she picked a piece and went that way. She began to think about cheese sandwiches.

This was really no wonder, as by now, though she didn't know it, the time was seven o'clock in the evening; she had been out for more than three hours, and she hadn't eaten very much dinner, anyway, because it was pig, which she would never touch. ('Pork,' said her mother every time; 'Pig,' said Rose obstinately.)

Still, on she went, noticing that her shadow was longer now; feeling the money in her pocket and thinking that if she came to a little shop, she'd buy an ice cream.

Apart from this, she had no plans: she just went on walking. Never had there been such a long and winding and deserted road; not even a cottage; not so much as a person on a bicycle.

– As a matter of fact, there really were a few cottages, but they stood behind high hedges, and Rose was either too short to see over, or happened to be looking at a snail or something at the time.

At last she came to a really main road, with cats' eyes, and a signpost that pointed to London one way, to Brighton another. She didn't want to go to either of these places, but by now her legs were so tired that they stumped along, it seemed, of their own accord, one after the other, as if they weren't hers at all. She was very hungry indeed, and started to eat grass, pulling out the juicy bits from the stems.

Back on the main road, there were a lot of cars; she kept to a newly-made cinder path at the side, hardly noticing that she was going the way to Brighton. What really attracted her was a house in the distance with – surely – an Ice Cream placard in front. She made her way doggedly towards it.

Cars were drawn up there; a little string of fairy-lights was already lit over the porch, making the roses look almost black, and the white paint very white. There was a tree with a circular seat round it, where a few bicycles leaned.

Although it was still daylight, the two downstairs windows of the house glowed rose-pink with a wonderful shine of bottles and coloured glass, like two enchanted caves at a pantomime.

Rose went in at the open door. A lot of men were standing about in the lamplight, talking loudly, with glasses or mugs in their hands. They didn't see her at first, but she gently pushed her way between them to the counter, where a fat man in a bright red waistcoat with brass buttons was wiping up a wet mark.

'Please can I have an ice cream?' She put down the very warm sixpence she had been holding.

The man looked down at her in surprise.

'Eh? Wait a minute, who sent you in here, missie?'

'Nobody.'

'You come off that coach out there? One of that party, are you?'

'No. But I've got sixpence. So please –'

'Look, you're not allowed in here, you know; this is a licensed house, you'll be getting me into trouble. Where are your mum and dad, then?'

'I don't know. I just came out for a walk.' Rose saw a heap of packets of potato crisps under a glass dome; her eyes suddenly filled with tears.

'Is this a pub?' she said; her voice quivered with disappointment. She knew that pubs were places where children had to wait outside. 'But the label said –'

'Ice creams, ah, but that's for the tea-garden only,' said the man. '– Which is now closed. Go on, now, you'd better hop it, else I shall cop it!' He grinned round for approval of this joke, but the other men either took no notice or stared blankly. Rose was trying very hard not to cry.

'Couldn't I even have some – some –', she looked at the crisps, but no more words would come. She struggled with her face, but it won, and the tears rolled down faster than her fist could stop them.

'Here, what's all this about? No call to cry – you ought to be home in bed, anyway; don't know what you mum's up to, sending you out a time like this –'

'She didn't send me!' wailed Rose, and this time the crying was no longer silent, but burst out into a real howl, such as her family would have recognised a mile away. She was crying partly for herself, partly because the man was so stupid and she just couldn't stand it.

This time, people really did look round with some interest.

'What's your name, dear?'

'Where d'you live?'

'Somebody ought to take her home, it'll be getting dark soon –'

They all crowded round with questions and suggestions; but Rose simply stood there with tears dripping all down the front of her dress and even on to the floor.

Suddenly a new voice spoke – it was a man who had only just come in.

''Allo, 'allo, 'allo, what's up? Somebody in trouble? Well, I'll be bothered! if it isn't the little lady what lost 'er doll! Here –' he gently shook her shoulder – 'remember me?'

Rose looked up, and saw a large moustache, a kind pink face, and a chewing jaw. Yes, it was the man with the cap, who had gone down the well! But even then, she couldn't stop crying straight away.

'Come on, now, mop 'em up,' he said, 'and tell us what you're a-doin' of 'ere, eh? We'd better step outside, though, the landlord's not allowed to let nippers into the bar, and we don't want to get 'im into trouble too, do we?'

'No,' wept Rose, and let him take her hand and lead her out to the grass patch in front.

'Come an' meet the Missus,' he said, and took her to a lorry drawn up under the trees.

The man-with-the-cap's wife was sitting in the front of the lorry, waiting for the beer he had meant to get her; but when she saw Rose she seemed to forget all about it; and by the time Rose had managed to tell them most of her story, and how she was lost, they were full of concern and said of course they'd take her home. But would she mind if they dropped the wife and their own nipper back at their place first, as it was well past that nipper's bedtime? – In fact all that needed to be done, they said, was to lift her out of the back of the lorry, where she was fast asleep, tucked up in an old eiderdown sewn up like a bag.

Rose was very much interested to see; she quite stopped crying, and the man lifted her up so that she could peer over the side.

'Is that her doll?' whispered Rose.

'That's right. That's Jessica, that is. And not to be called Jessie, if you please.'

'What's your little girl's own name?'

'Dawn,' said the man proudly. 'Dawn Elizabeth Edie, after the Queen and 'er grandma.'

'How nice,' said Rose. He lifted her up into the front seat, where she settled between him and his wife.

'You'll be 'ungry,' said the Missus.

'Yes. Very.'

'Poor little mite. I'll get 'er something,' she murmured over Rose's head – 'soon as we're 'ome; it won't take a minute.'

'They'll be worryin' about 'er, I should reckon,' said the man.

'I'll just get our Dawn tucked up, and we'll 'ave a bite in no time,' said the comfortable Missus.

So that was how Rose came to have scrambled egg with cheese, cocoa, four slices of new white bread and home-made strawberry jam.

She could never understand why, when the man finally delivered her home, her mother cried.

'Aren't you *pleased* to see me?' she asked – which only made her mother cry the more.

As for the police, Rose never even knew they had come into it at all. Louisa and Japhet had strict instructions to say nothing. All the same, it was made very clear that Rose was never, never to go off like that again.

– But when, a few days later, a parcel arrived, containing a golden-haired doll, labelled 'Jessica's Twin, with love from Dawn' – Rose wondered if it wasn't perhaps worth it after all?

Chapter Fifteen

Louisa had given up – or at any rate had determined to give up – all idea of finding Captain Noah.

'He's just unlucky,' she said, 'like the Old Man of the Sea.'

But it was strange how dead everything now seemed. The one bright spot in life, at present, was that they had at last heard from the Pony Society; the letter said they could keep Jo after all, but would they please be very careful in future? Louisa herself wrote to say they would.

A man came to seal up the well with cement; their father spent hours gathering up charred branches in the wood; their mother said she might as well look upon her engagement ring as lost, for good and all. Rose was too much wrapped up in the new golden-haired doll to think of anything else; she nagged Louisa into helping her make clothes for it. She called it Eve, 'because it's the opposite of Dawn'.

That old boot lay in the chicken house, forgotten; the biscuit tin of paper was pushed to the back of the airing-cupboard by relays of ironing; Japhet was too busy with other things to think much more about that wooden compass.

Yet it was Japhet who made the great discovery.

Anyway, the discovery. You might think it great or you might not.

He was to go, one evening during the week, to explain to Mr Cuthbertson about the TV set.

'What, alone?' he asked in dismay.

'Yes,' said his father, who had decided that it would be part of Japhet's punishment to have to go and confess by himself.

Naturally, Japhet kept putting it off. One evening he had been given some extra sums to do; he set to work on them with extraordinary industry. The next evening, he didn't feel very well; the next, deciding that Oats must be taken for a really good walk, he went to the gipsy's old camp 'to do a bit of sleuthing about that ring.'

'He might have hidden it,' he said, 'and be coming back.'

'He'd have come by now,' said Louisa.

'He'd wait till suspicion had died down.'

'Nonsense! Anyway, he'd never get far with it; the police are bound to trace him, and if he tries to sell it, they'll know.'

'How will they?' asked Rose.

'They have ways,' Louisa said vaguely; her faith in the police was not to be easily shaken.

'Anyway,' said Japhet, '*some*body's been at the camp lately.'

'How d'you know?'

'There was a fire.'

'Goodness, I hope you stamped it out!' said their mother.

'I didn't think I'd better. There was something cooking on it.'

'What?' asked Rose.

'Two sausages.'

'Ugh! Pig!'

'Gipsies would be more likely to have beef ones,' said Louisa calmly; 'they're cheaper.'

'They were all black on one side, so I turned them over. Then I cleared off,' Japhet explained. 'I didn't particularly *want* to meet that gipsy. Besides, Oats was a bit interested in the sausages. – But mind you, I'd had a good look all round. They've left an awful lot of junk; I should say there are things somebody'd be quite glad of. I mean, a tramp. Well, there's an old spring mattress, and half a chair, and a saucepan that *could* be mended –'

'Tramps don't sit on chairs, anyway,' said Louisa. 'By the way, we haven't had any more of them coming to the door, have we – perhaps that one who had coffee instead of tea didn't make a sign after all.'

'I certainly hope not,' said their mother, 'we've had quite enough to cope with lately. If a tramp came now, I wouldn't make him coffee or anything else. And Japhet, you're to go to Mr Cuthbertson's tomorrow evening without fail, do you understand? He'll be coming back with our old set repaired before we know where we are, and then what should we do? We *must* tell him first.'

So Japhet got off the bus, with a sinking heart, at the stop near the electric shop.

Slowly he walked up to the door. He paused at the window to look at a new TV that was on show there, working. There was Wimbledon tennis going on; normally Japhet took little interest in this, but now he stood gazing as if it were the most fascinating thing in the world. He was too deeply lost in his own thoughts to notice a figure draw near and stand by his side.

Slowly, reluctantly, he pushed open the door of the shop. A youth in a grey cotton dust-coat came forward to serve him.

'Yes, sir? Good afternoon.' They were always very polite in Cuthbertson's. There was even a carpet inside, most unusual for a village shop, and they had recently had a sound-proof box made where you could listen to gramophone records. There was a radio playing now, as well as the TV in the window; light tea-time music oozed round the electric fires and hair-dryers hanging on the glossy walls.

How could Japhet say, here, in these smooth and civilised surroundings, 'I've shot your telly'?

But that's just what he did say, in those very words.

The youth in the grey coat stared.

'I beg your pardon?' he said. Japhet told him again.

' 'Ang on,' said the astonished youth, forgetting his shop voice. He disappeared into the back quarters; Japhet waited for the terrible descent of Mr Cuthbertson, whom he had never actually seen.

He waited for what seemed like hours: in fact, it was two whole minutes before Mr Cuthbertson came.

He ambled forward, wiping his moustache: he had just been finishing his tea.

'Now then, what's all this?' he said, and pushed his spectacles to the tip of his nose, the better to peer at Japhet.

'I didn't think it was loaded,' muttered Japhet desperately, 'I really didn't. I would never have –'

'Hold on a minute, hold on,' said Mr Cuthbertson, 'let's get this straight. Now first of all, who *are* you?'

It was Japhet's turn to be astonished. Surely that youth had had time to tell the facts – the worst of them? But no, it seemed he hadn't: or was Mr Cuthbertson just pretending, tormenting his victim, playing with him, making him tell it all over again just to see him squirm?

Japhet looked at him. He didn't *look* that kind of a man at all; in fact he looked altogether different from what you'd expect, going by the smartness of the shop. Someone hard, brisk, polished, go-ahead – that was the picture Japhet had had in mind. But here was a big, vague, gentle, pale-brown walrus of a man, with small tired eyes and hands that were surely too puffed and swollen with rheumatism to be able to hold a screw-driver, let alone mend a fuse? You could more easily imagine him as a greengrocer, fumbling with potatoes, or as an old-fashioned baker, making great plaited loaves for harvest festivals. TV sets and long-playing jazz records seemed all out of keeping.

Japhet was certainly less scared than he had expected to be, as he told his story. He even put in what the Black Riders had been doing, at the moment when he fired the shot.

Mr Cuthbertson listened attentively.

When the story was finished, he adjusted his spectacles, folded his arms and gave Japhet a long stare. Japhet quailed.

'Will it be *terribly* expensive?' he said. 'Will we have to pay for the whole set, or d'you think it could be repaired? I've got about fifteen shillings,' he added meekly, 'which I was saving up for something. But that doesn't matter now.'

Then Mr Cuthbertson said a most extraordinary thing. Of all the remarks Japhet might have expected, furious or threatening or just coldly stern, this remark wouldn't have occurred to him in his wildest dreams.

Mr Cuthbertson said: 'Did you get him?'

'Who?'

'The one you were shooting. Was it the thin one with the moustache?'

'No. The fat one with the scar,' said Japhet, dazed.

'I'd like to get that thin one,' Mr Cuthbertson said, narrowing his eyes. 'I reckon he's always the cause of the trouble. I wouldn't trust him from here to the shop next-door. I *hate* that thin one!' he added vehemently.

'Do you watch the Black Riders, then?' Japhet wasn't sure if Mr Cuthbertson was pulling his leg, and would suddenly turn nasty after all.

'Regular,' said Mr Cuthbertson. 'Never miss. I like it when they go round that rock, don't you – my daughter, she says it's always the same old rock, every time, but then she don't appreciate Westerns. Did you see the one where he stood up on top and lassoed 'em as they came galloping by underneath? That was good. But I wish you'd aimed at the thin one, though.'

'I'm afraid it went right through the glass,' said Japhet. 'The bullet must be inside somewhere.' He was beginning to feel that it was he who had to take charge of the situation; Mr Cuthbertson seemed slightly mad. Or to put it more kindly, he was even more of a TV enthusiast than Japhet himself – but

136

between them, they had a shot set on their hands.

'Well, we'll have to get the doctor to her, shan't we?' said Mr Cuthbertson. 'You tell your Dad to keep the patient quiet till I get out there.'

'It can't be anything *but* quiet,' said Japhet. 'It's dead.'

Mr Cuthbertson raised a large protesting paw.

'Never use that word,' he said; 'while there's a current there's life. I'll be round tomorrow.'

'There'll be a new glass front needed –' began Japhet doubtfully.

'Of course: I've no doubt it'll be a major surgical operation. Three o'clock. – What's the matter?'

'Nothing; only I thought you'd be awfully cross.'

Mr Cuthbertson shook his head. 'My daughter,' he said, 'now if you'd have seen *her*, it'd be different. Mind you, she's the business woman; credit where credit's due. It was her idea, all this lark of the plastic walls and the gramophone hole and getting us fancied up. Contemp'ry, she calls it. You won't get anywhere today unless you're contemp'ry, she says. Well, I dare say she's right. Though I can't feel at home in it myself; that's why I stick to my workshop.'

'But at any rate, you can have the telly on all day long if you want to.'

'Not when the daughter's around,' said Mr Cuthbertson, winking. 'She's a stickler for the business. Quite right, of course; if it wasn't for her, I'd still be spreading sawdust on the floor. – Though I tell you one thing –' and he leaned forward to Japhet like a conspirator – 'she don't know AC from DC! So you see!' He stood back, smiling gently in triumph. 'We've all got to do our bit,' he concluded, 'that's what it comes to. – And as for you, you know what's *your* trouble, don't you?'

'Well,' said Japhet, 'there have been such a lot of them lately.'

'Look here –' and Mr Cuthbertson picked up a light bulb and held it for a moment in the testing-socket. It lit up. 'See that? – Which is caused by what? By electricity, you'll say. All right, granted. But what's electricity? Tell me that!' Japhet shook his head. 'You see? It's a mystery. By the light of which I say, if you believe in electricity, you can believe in anything. Well, why not? If this isn't magic, what is?' He made the light flicker on, off, on, off, on. . . .

'I never thought of it like that,' said Japhet.

'No, you wouldn't. It's what I was saying: *your* trouble is, you *don't* think, hardly at all.' He tapped Japhet between the eyes with the blunt dry end of his forefinger. 'What you do in there,' he went on, 'is not thinking. It's just imagination.'

'But imagining *is* thinking, isn't it?' Japhet felt he was getting out of his depth.

'To you, yes; to me, yes; not to *them* –' and Mr Cuthbertson cocked a thumb towards the shop window and the street. 'Why do *their* sets go wrong? Do they throw things at 'em? Do they start kicking 'em? Fighting 'em? *Shooting* 'em? Not they. And goodness knows they've cause enough! Mind you, it's as well they don't because in that event I'd never have the heart to charge the proper amount. When it's imagination, I reckon we ought to be glad, not stick it on the bill. – Course, I'll have to charge you *some*thing,' he added, 'or the daughter'll be on the war-path.'

'Well,' said Japhet after a pause during which Mr Cuthbertson seemed to be dreaming behind his moustache. '– Well, I think I'd better go now.'

'Gawpers!' shouted Mr Cuthbertson suddenly, bringing his fist down on the counter. Japhet jumped. 'Just gawpers, that's all they are! What do they care if it's murder going on, or that Black Rider's up to his dirty tricks again –'

'The thin one?'

'Yes – but who cares? It's breeding the feeling out of people, that's what it's doing,' he went on earnestly. 'Listen: now I'll tell *you* something. I once chucked a teapot right through the first seventeen-inch screen I ever had, because of the way Dirk Dangerwood was threatening some poor Indians. I couldn't stand it, I just couldn't stand it – so smash! Right through!'

'Was there tea in it?' asked Japhet.

'Just the dregs; I'd had my three cups. But honestly, the way those Indians used to get treated, it'd make you cry. They're better nowadays, a bit.'

'Did you repair it?'

'What? Oh, the set! Yes, yes, I got her trimmed up all right. Expect we'll do the same with yours, too.'

'It's yours really,' Japhet reminded him. 'You lent it to us while –'

'Oh yes, so I did,' said Mr Cuthbertson vaguely. He was clearly no business man; even Japhet could see that.

'Anyway, we'll have a look at her tomorrow. You'll miss "Ranger Patrol", though,' he added with a look of great concern. 'I don't see what we can do about

139

that. I'd ask you round here, but my daughter'll be back tonight, and –'

'That's quite all right,' said Japhet hastily. He didn't want to have to explain that he wouldn't be allowed out at that time anyway. 'I'll tell my father you're coming tomorrow.'

Mr Cuthbertson nodded and pulled out a small black pipe, which he started to fill, pressing down the tobacco surprisingly delicately with his great misshapen fingers. The youth in the coat came back; Japhet said goodbye.

This time, the bell on the shop door sounded gay, not grim. Japhet felt as if a dentist had given him fish and chips instead of the drill. Perhaps this meant good luck, at last!

Chapter Sixteen

The figure was still standing on the pavement outside.

Japhet realised, now, that he had half-seen it before; but he had been too worried to notice any details.

Now he felt so pleased that he would have spoken to anybody.

'Afternoon,' he said. 'Nice day.'

The figure seemed to hitch itself together; slowly, with a kind of hard-breathing shuffle, it turned round.

Curly grizzled beard; brown face; bright blue eyes: that was Japhet's first impression. He didn't notice the dirt till later.

'Come far?' he asked cheerfully.

The tramp gazed at him, or through him; it was hard to decide which. But without a word.

'It's a nice shop,' said Japhet. 'It's nice inside too. Which way are you going?'

Still no answer. 'Well,' said Japhet, 'Goodbye.'

Then suddenly the tramp started to mutter furiously, in a very deep voice. Japhet couldn't understand a word he said; he talked as if he had a mouthful of beard but no teeth. – Or perhaps, Japhet thought, he hadn't spoken to anyone for years, and had forgotten how. Anyway, all you could do was smile and nod and stare.

The muttering didn't seem to be actually unfriendly – more, Japhet thought, excited, as if the man had some long-pent up grievance, and had at last found a listener. He waved one arm as he spoke; Japhet noticed that it was tattooed: he could see the initial 'A' – and what looked like a ship on curly waves.

Suddenly the thought hit him like a shot out of a gun.

Could it be? Was it possible? The name on that compass – wasn't it 'Alberta'? Well, 'A' for – but wait: hadn't the Gillingses said the Captain was short-sighted, nearly blind? Then he wouldn't be looking at TV in a shop window. Japhet glanced up: those bright blue eyes looked straight over his head; but they might have been watching a dog up the road. He glanced down: those feet! Surely there had never been such big ones – big enough, even, for that colossal boot in the chicken house!

Japhet plucked up his courage; it was now or never. 'I say,' he said, 'is your name Noah?'

Suddenly the tramp seemed to stare straight at him. Another outburst of muttering, and he turned away, still talking to himself all down the street. People looked, and shrugged, and looked the other way. Just another tramp.

But Japhet, keeping a safe distance, followed him.

By the last house in the village the tramp stopped. Japhet stopped too, and pretended to be looking at some flowers in a front garden.

The tramp seemed to be rummaging about in the hedge. It crossed Japhet's mind that he might have hidden something there, something he didn't want to carry all the time.

The hedge belonged to somebody's cottage; Japhet heard a warning voice shout from an open window;

they were telling the tramp to go away.

He did; but he had found what he wanted.

It was a white stick.

'But why hide it?' Louisa protested for the fourth time. 'And why, if he's blind, was he looking in the television shop?'

'Perhaps he was just listening,' suggested Rose.

'What, to Wimbledon?'

'Some people do just turn off the picture and listen. When they can't stand it. I've heard them say so. Anyway, I quite like those pings of tennis balls.'

'Anyway,' she added 'perhaps he was only *pretending* to be blind.'

Louisa and Japhet looked at each other: really, Rose was getting quite sharp. The idea appealed specially to Japhet, because it suggested mystery or even crime.

'By *why*?' Louisa frowned. 'After all, if he wanted people to give him something, he'd pretend to be blind *in* the village, not outside it. Besides, Captain Noah actually was nearly blind, we know that.'

'But he didn't want to admit it – they told you, the Gillingses did – so now he goes about pretending he can see. But somebody probably told him he *must* have the white stick for the roads where there's no pavement, so cars can be careful. So he keeps the stick for when he's out of the village!' Japhet was getting quite excited.

'But he'd have to have carried it *through* the village to have got it to the other end,' Louisa objected. 'That is, if he was travelling straight on.'

'But he wasn't!' Japhet hissed triumphantly. 'He'd just come in for a visit – from the gipsy camp place and back!'

'Are you sure?'

'Yes. I followed him there. That was his fire I saw the other day.'

'And his sausages.' Rose pulled a face.

'Still,' said Louisa, 'I don't suppose for one moment it *is* Captain Noah. Why should it be? It's just ridiculous. He's probably not even in England, if he's alive at all.'

She must resist the temptation to go back to the old search. And although it had started only a few weeks ago, it really did seem old now; a dusty story from a dusty hole in the ceiling. Far away and absurd; she marvelled that she could ever have been so childish. No wonder she hadn't heard from that Mr Glover at the museum; he had probably thought she was mad, and had thrown the letter into the waste paper basket, with bits of rejected pottery and faded labels that had had to be replaced.

All the same, it was difficult not to be just slightly interested in Japhet's tramp. From the description, he did fit her picture of the Captain: tall, brown, blue-eyed – she would have put in the tattoo mark, too, if she had thought of it. The only thing that worried her was the muttering. She had imagined a deep voice, yes – but it was horrible to think that if this was, by any remote chance, the Captain, he had become just a jabbering old idiot.

But nonsense: she pulled herself together. The tramp was *not* the Captain, and that was that. And she had heard her father say that most tramps were, in fact, a bit queer in the head.

He had muttered to himself all the way to the gipsy's

place, Japhet said.

'Then he sat down and started cooking. So I came away. He'd got something wrapped up in newspaper; he put it in the frying pan.'

'What, the newspaper?' asked Rose.

'Silly ass!'

'Well, you said –'

'Oh, go to bed!' said Japhet.

'I say!' he whispered later as Louisa passed his bedroom door.

'Ssh! What?'

'Telly again tomorrow! Smashing!' Japhet was hugging himself with pleasure. He still felt on top of the world with relief about the way Mr Cuthbertson had reacted. Being Japhet, he had even stopped thinking it was strange. All that mattered was that things were going to be all right – so why bother? Of course, it would cost a *bit*, but nothing like what his father had feared. And as to the matter of the actual repair, and whether it could be done, Japhet had complete faith in Mr Cuthbertson. In spite of those puffy hands. In spite of that drooping moustache, that unbusiness-like manner, those improbable remarks. Japhet had a hunch that where electricity was concerned, Mr Cuthbertson was a kind of wizard.

The hunch turned out to be perfectly right.

The next afternoon, they all came home from school to find Mr Cuthbertson squatting massively on the sitting-room floor, surrounded by tubes, screws, nuts, bolts, valves, wires, plugs, and every conceivable kind of small tool.

'I've never seen the inside of a television before,' said Rose, wide-eyed.

'Have a good look; perhaps you never will again.' Mr Cuthbertson gave her a quick glance over the top of his spectacles; it was as if he was saying 'Do you appreciate these marvels? Are you one of Us?' Apparently he decided that Rose did, and was; she certainly looked impressed. Anyway, he invited her to sit down, if she could find a space, and hold his screwdriver.

'Then I'll know where it is. I'm inclined to sit on things,' he added confidentially; and looking at his expanse, Rose thought it would be difficult for him not to.

'Shall I take him a cup of tea?' Louisa asked her mother.

'The number of cups of tea, coffee, cocoa I've made lately, really! – Yes, and ask him if he takes sugar.'

Louisa put the things on a tray, with a rather old rock cake she found oddly, in the fridge.

'Rose put that there,' explained her mother. 'It's for her dolls. I wasn't to move it.'

'They'll have to have bread and butter,' Louisa said firmly.

'She'll make a fuss.' – But Louisa found Rose far too happily absorbed to notice what was on Mr Cuthbertson's saucer. She was sitting with the screwdriver in one hand, some screws in the other, and several lengths of wire and flex festooned around her neck. Japhet was peering at the innards of the TV; from time to time he asked 'Is she going to be all right?' or 'How's she doing now?' – just as if he were watching an operation

146

on a relative.

Mr Cuthbertson answered not a word; he just breathed heavily, and occasionally whistled between his teeth. Sometimes he signed to Rose for a nut or a screw; she was getting quite good at knowing what he wanted.

He paused to drink a mouthful of tea; little drops of sweat glistened all over his domed forehead. He let the rest of the tea get cold, and ignored the rock cake; the atmosphere was intense, concentrated, as if this were not so much a job as a mission. Rose felt it, and sat quiet, doing her part; Japhet felt it, and was all agog for results, which he thought might happen at any minute now. Louisa, too, felt it, and stood in the background with the sense of being in the presence of genius.

– Which was just what their father said Cuthbertson must be, when he came home to find the TV in perfect working order, new glass, finely-adjusted picture, sound booming out as usual. He turned it down, but although it was only a washing-powder interview, Japhet was most indignant.

'Nearly a whole week without the telly, and now I can't even *hear* it!'

'Well, whose fault was it in the first place, I'd like to know? I call that the limit!'

Really, Louisa thought, the way Japhet could forget things. But at least he had the grace to look a little shamefaced now. 'The bill's on top,' he said.

'He didn't want to leave one,' Louisa told her father, 'but mother said we ought to know the worst.'

They all sat tight while their father tore open the envelope.

'How much?' asked Louisa.

'A lot?' said Rose.

'More than you thought?' Japhet was a little nervous.

Their father paused and took a deep breath. ' "Supply of new parts, no charge," ' he read. ' "As set is coming back to shop".'

'But –' their mother began; their father waved her aside. ' "Repairs",' he went on, – and took another breath – ' "Sixpence".'

'Sixpence!' Louisa gasped.

'Sixpence!' Japhet said with a dawning grin.

'Sixpence – that's not *very* much, is it?' asked Rose placidly.

'The man must be mad!' said their mother. '*Sixpence* for repairing it! But he was here all afternoon! You should have seen the state of this room!'

'And he tidied it all up, too,' Louisa remarked.

'Wait a minute,' their father said, 'a bit more: "Bus fare: To you, 4d. From You, 4d. Total 1/2." Then it says: "Hope Japhet enjoys B. Rs. tomorrow. But better not do it again – not even the thin one." '

'What are the B.Rs.?' their mother asked.

'The Black Riders,' said Japhet, '– and I know what he means.'

'It's more than we do. Is that all?'

'No – there's one more bit: it's squiggled down here at the bottom.' Their father frowned. 'Looks like "Please pay me, not Miss C." '

'That'll be his daughter,' said Japhet knowingly. 'He doesn't want her to know he's charged so little; she'd be cross.'

'So should I be, if I were in her shoes,' their mother

remarked. 'How on earth can he run his business like that?'

'He can't,' said their father. 'If he went around doing this to everyone, he'd be broke.'

'But why *us*?' Louisa asked.

'Well, not everyone shoots their telly,' said Japhet.

'Whatever did you tell him? Did you say we were paupers or something?'

'I simply said I'd shot it,' said Japhet patiently. 'And he told me he once threw a teapot at one. So I suppose he thinks we're quits.'

'I don't see any quits about it,' Louisa said. 'It just sounds madder and madder to me.'

'There wasn't any tea in it,' Japhet explained.

'Anyway,' said their father, 'we'll have to pay him more than this. Well, a bit more. He may be an eccentric, but that's no reason why we should take advantage of him. I'll go and see him tomorrow.'

'But I don't understand: *what* teapot?' said Rose, worried and two remarks behind as usual. The conversation about the bill had been above her head, but she thought she ought to get the teapot straight. 'Japhet, what teapot? Whose teapot?' she complained.

But Japhet was far away with Buck Barehide, which had just begun. Together with Buck he stalked round a log cabin in the Rockies, all else forgotten.

Rose realised that the teapot was one of those things no-one would ever explain; so she went off to give her dolls their medicine.

The next day was Saturday again; a very dull Saturday, Louisa thought, remembering last week when she had been all set for London and Somerset House. What ages ago that seemed! Rose getting lost, the fire, the house being broken into – a lot had happened in a very short time. She felt almost a different person from the one she had been last Saturday. As if she had grown up. That was probably the result of being completely sensible, at last, about the Captain. And the weather had changed too; it was still warm, but it had turned grey. No more sunbathing; no more looking up into a sky of such an unlikely blue that you could all too easily imagine unlikely things happening beneath it. Louisa was firmly back to earth; she had never, as far as she remembered, had one foot off it for so long.

She spent the morning giving Oats a shampoo on the lawn. In the afternoon she let Rose come with her for a cycle ride, and they had ice lollies at the little shop. It was always just 'the little shop' to them, because it wasn't in the village at all, but almost isolated at a cross-roads in the other direction, with nothing but two cottages, a bus stop and a letter-box near it. They liked the little shop, partly because it was always open on early-closing day; partly because it had really everything, stuffed or stacked or hung in so small a space: potatoes, hair-grips, butter and buckets and hobnailed boots – yet there were also all the latest kinds of things in packets, too, with a notice written in ink on the end of an old shoe box: 'As Advertised on TV'.

Rose wanted a marshmallow thing on a yellow wafer, with hundreds and thousands on the top and coconut whiskers all round. It was only three-halfpence, so Louisa paid for it, realising with a slight shock how completely she herself had grown out of such things.

She supposed that at Rose's age she would have thought it nice. Feeling more grown-up than ever, she actually didn't have any sweets herself, because she had been on the weighing machine in the bathroom the night before. She and Georgia were having a private competition to see who could lose more weight before the end of term. They were both on the large side, but Georgia was lucky, because her mother was always slimming too, so there were sure to be starch-reduced rolls and things in the house. Louisa's mother had bouts of going on a diet, but they never lasted long, and then she would go and buy one of those malt loaves, or suddenly make a cake, or have to get an ice cream block at the last minute because she'd forgotten to put the baked apples in early enough.

Louisa and Rose cycled slowly home, sucking their lollies. The roads were grey, the hedges were thick and seemed to give off a dull warmth; the hard green blackberries were dusty from passing cars. It was Saturday afternoon and there was nothing to hurry for, nothing to get excited about; just an ordinary ride home to tea.

But why was Japhet out in front of the house there, signalling?

Louisa saw him first; Rose was dreaming along looking at a bit of cow-parsley that had caught in her wheel. She didn't stop to take it out; she liked the small twanging noise it made.

'Whatever's the matter with Japhet?' said Louisa. 'He doesn't generally come out to meet us. Something must be wrong.'

It quickly crossed her mind that either her mother or

her father or Oats or Jo might be ill; perhaps there had been an accident. Japhet was waving frantically, as if to tell them to hurry up. Then he came running along the road, towards them, with Oats at his heels. Louisa mentally ticked off Oats as all right, anyway. Rose laughed at the way he bounced over tufts of grass, as if he were going along on springs.

'Perhaps there's been another fire,' she said hopefully. She was still very sad about having missed that one the other night.

'Japhet wouldn't look so pleased,' said Louisa, who could see his face now. 'Besides, there's no smoke.'

'Perhaps they've caught the gipsy and got the ring.'

'Whatever's he pointing at?' Louisa frowned. Japhet was dancing about, silently mouthing something, and making energetic signs in the direction of the back of their house.

'What on *earth*. . . . ?' Louisa got off her bike; Japhet's face was scarlet.

'Whatever's the matter?' she asked.

Japhet glowed and shone.

'I've got him!' he said.

'Who?'

'The Captain!'

'How? Where?'

It looked for a moment as if Japhet would burst.

'In the chicken house!' he shouted, and raced that way.

Chapter Seventeen

'It's all right,' said Louisa. 'He won't bite. Oats! Stop that!

'Growling means hallo really,' Rose explained.

'I'll get you some of Jo's hay to sit on,' said Japhet.

'What would you like for tea?' asked Rose.

The tramp – if he really was a tramp – sat and stared towards each of them in turn as they spoke. His blue eyes looked hard and bright: not so much *at* you, Louisa thought, as just over your shoulder. She was almost sure he was blind. But not quite sure.

'Don't worry,' she said, 'we won't tell anyone you're here. We'd get into trouble ourselves if we did.' But at the same time she was wondering what on earth they ought to do. Japhet seemed perfectly happy – just stood there, beaming, triumphant, not thinking of the future at all.

'You see, our mother's a bit worried about tra –' began Rose, and had a kick from Japhet before she could get out the 'mps'.

'Anyway,' she said, putting a brave face on it, 'I could bring you some of my bread and butter.'

'And I dare say some milk,' said Japhet, 'if not cake.'

'If there's both, which will you have, brown or white?'

The man stared past them harder still. It gave

Louisa a queer feeling; it was as if he could see something in the distance that no-one else could see.

She studied him cautiously. He was certainly all that she had imagined the Captain to be – and yet now, face to face and in the flesh, there was something, she couldn't see what, but something that was not quite right. Would the Captain, for instance, ever have let himself get so dirty? Of course, a blind man couldn't see to wash. (Though you *could* wash in the dark; she'd had to, that time all the lights had fused.) But would the Captain have sat there so animal-like, so dumb? She didn't think so. And would he have let himself be led here by Japhet without a word either of protest or recognition? Wouldn't his feet have known the very stones and ruts of the path up to the house, even if he couldn't see it? Then why hadn't he said something, given some sign? Or perhaps he had lost his memory? But she couldn't, or wouldn't, believe that. At least, not this house, she told herself; he would never forget that; not completely.

'You can sleep here,' Japhet was saying, 'I'll fetch an old blanket.'

'But what will they say?' whispered Rose, meaning her mother and father.

'They won't know, they never come here.'

'They do in the winter.' She looked at the block where her father sawed up logs.

'What's that got to do with it?' said Japhet, who would never hold himself responsible for what happened next week, let alone next winter. 'Shan't be long,' he told the tramp (or Captain). 'You just stay there.'

The Captain (or tramp) seemed to watch him, or

rather to watch his shadow, as he went out of the flimsy wooden door. Rose was keeping an eye on Oats, who was keeping an eye on the newcomer with comments of gruff suspicion. Louisa surveyed them all: she seemed to be the only one of them, except perhaps Oats, who was actually thinking this thing out.

First, was the tramp the Captain? Or just a poor wandering half-wit? Or a cunning impostor, pretending to know less than he did? And how could they find any of these things out?

Second, if he really was by any wild chance the Captain – she wouldn't let herself believe it, but suppose he *was* – what then? What were they supposed to do with him? She realised, now, that the search had been a fantastic kind of game – well-meaning, perhaps, but fantastic. Of course, she had tried to be efficient about it, and practical – but she had never really quite believed in it: she couldn't have, or she would have thought more about the actual consequences. It was one thing to be on a quest; it was quite another to find what you were looking for. Come to think of it, Louisa reflected, the whole point of quests was that people were *on* them. What happened afterwards was never in the books.

Of course, if this were the true Captain, they must see that he got his rightful inheritance from that uncle. But how terrible if he weren't, and they led him to make a false claim! The lawyers would find out, and he might look pretty silly – which, if it got into the papers, would be almost as bad.

Japhet came back with the blanket. 'Tea's ready,' he said. 'Now you stay here, won't you; don't go away, and we'll bring you some food. There's chocolate cake!' He spoke to the man as if he were a big baby; the tramp mumbled but showed no sign of moving.

They could hardly sit through their tea. Louisa and Japhet had told Rose on no account whatever to mention anything about the chicken house. 'It'd be fatal,' said Japhet in a dramatic whisper.

'Shall I get a paper bag to put some bread and butter in?' asked Rose.

'No,' said Louisa firmly. 'You'd never be able to do it without somebody seeing.'

'You'd give the whole show away,' Japhet agreed. 'We can snaffle some stuff afterwards; we can offer to clear the things away.'

'That'd look a bit funny,' Louisa remarked, 'considering.'

Their mother noticed that they ate less than usual, and put it down to the muggy weather.

'It's so close,' she said, 'it feels like a storm again – in which case the cricket'll be over early, and perhaps your father will have time to put up that line in the chicken house.'

'No!' Japhet nearly shot out of his chair.

'Not in the chicken house, surely?' said Louisa, keeping her voice steady.

'What line?' Rose asked.

'Oh, he's going to put up a clothes line in there for me; it'll make quite a good drying-room for wet weather; I thought of it ages ago and kept forgetting to tell him. And I do hate damp things hanging round indoors.'

'Oh, I don't!'

'Nor do I!'

'I rather like the smell!'

'The chicken house is so dirty!'

'Awful!'

'The clothes would stink in there!'

Their mother looked at them in astonishment as they all spoke at once.

'Well, well, well!' she said. 'I've never heard you all so unanimous. Anybody'd think you were hiding something out there!'

Rose saved the situation by asking 'What's You Nanny –'

'– Mouse,' said Japhet; even he was blushing a bit. But by the time Rose had got the word right, they were back to their normal colour, and their mother thought no more about it. Her short memory had its advantages.

The Captain (or tramp) sat eating a piece of chocolate swiss roll. On the earth floor by his side was a half bottle of milk; Japhet had pinched that from the fridge as he often did; no-one would think twice about it. The tramp (Captain) had already got through three Marmite sandwiches and one jam one; these wouldn't be missed either, as left-overs generally did disappear in due course, eaten by anyone passing the pantry door, or given to Oats or the birds.

The man ate in silence; he had wrapped the old blanket round his legs, and reclined on a layer of hay, looking very comfortable.

'*I* know!' said Japhet quietly. 'I'll show him the compass!'

'He won't be able to see it,' Louisa pointed out.

'He can tell by feel. Blind people do.'

'He may just pretend to recognise it, when he doesn't really.'

'Why on earth should he? You're just jealous because *you* didn't find him!'

'I'm not!' Louisa was indignant. 'I simply don't want to do anything silly, that's all.'

'Well, we've got to find out somehow. If he *is* Noah, he's bound to recognise the compass. If he isn't, he probably won't know what it is at all.' And Japhet went off to get it.

But the result was doubtful, either way. The man took it, fingered it all over, appeared to like it, muttered, nodded, and handed it back.

Japhet and Louisa looked at each other questioningly. Louisa shook her head. She had watched the man's fingers pass over the letters of the word 'Alberta' – and pass too casually, she thought. Yet he had tapped the thing, and laid it flat on his knees, as if he knew what it was. If only he would speak in a way they could understand!

But it was Rose who remembered the one simple thing they had forgotten.

'Of course! The boot! Where is it?'

'Here.' Japhet pulled it out of a corner. It looked very dusty, and more enormous than ever.

'It's like Cinderella the other way round,' said Rose. 'Not who's got a small enough foot, but who's got a big enough one.'

'In that case we ought to put out a notice for all the tramps in the kingdom,' said Japhet.

'You dare!' Louisa threatened, thinking of her mother's reaction to the appearance of a stream of tramps lining up, each with one bare foot.

'It's a *very* big boot,' said Rose. It really was. But however gigantic, Louisa thought, it mustn't be regarded as absolute proof.

'In one book, the second Ugly Sister cuts off her toes,' Rose remarked. 'But it wasn't allowed.'

'Nor is padding!' said Japhet, approaching the figure on the hay. 'No extra socks, no bits of rag – no newspaper!' he added, remembering that he had once seen a thing on TV about how down-and-outs sometimes slept with newspapers round their feet.

The man was apparently staring straight ahead of him, towards the old horseshoe stuck on a nail on the opposite wall. Japhet said politely (Louisa had never heard him so polite) that they would like him to try on a new boot.

'You mean an old one,' said Rose.

'Second-hand,' said Louisa.

The blanket was pulled away; slowly, with scrabbling fingers, the man unlaced and pulled off his own boot – which was certainly as old as the one they were about to offer. Inside the boot was what had once been a sock. A very yellow and dirty big toe peered through the end. Rose drew back, and said she could see all right from the door, thank you.

The man put on the boot from the well.

Japhet danced about in ecstasy.

'It fits! It fits!' he yelled.

But Louisa, determined to do the thing properly, knelt down and felt the toe, as they did in shoe shops. Where did the big one come to? There? Or there? Or right down to the end? The leather was so hardened that it was difficult to tell.

'You'd better stand up,' she said, 'and try walking on it.'

Trailing bits of hay, the man limped up and down the chicken house; thump, clop; thump, clop; thump, — pause to feel as Japhet guided him where to turn round — clop. The unevenness of the boots made him sound like a cripple. Louisa was quite glad when he sat down again.

'His foot does seem *nearly* to fill it,' she said.

'Of course it does!' said Japhet. 'It's all right, isn't it?' he shouted in the man's ear, because being blind made a person seem deaf too. 'Quite comfortable?' He started to ease the boot off, but the man stopped him.

And then, for the first time, and to their amazement, their visitor spoke two distinct and unmistakeable words. Looking, as it seemed, straight at Japhet, and holding the huge boot in his huge brown hand, he said quite clearly:

'Where's pair?'

They stood gazing at him. It was as if Oats or one of Derek's pigs had suddenly spoken. Or as if a Chinaman had burst into cockney, or a bird had barked.

'Other boot!' said the man just as clearly, raising his voice.

'*We* haven't got it,' Japhet said.

'We thought *you* might of,' Rose added. '– Well, Cinderella did,' she grumbled as Louisa gave her a look.

'It was in the well; just the one, I'm afraid,' Japhet said apologetically. He was in half a mind to put in about the dog's skull, but thought it might be too upsetting. He himself would be very much upset if anyone confronted him with Oats's skull – let alone when he was down-and-out and had only been given one boot.

'But your toes *do* reach the end, don't they?' he said in an encouraging voice. 'We never thought anybody's would, you know!'

The man slowly let go of the boot; his face hardened, and he lapsed back into his old muttering; they couldn't understand a word, but it sounded rather unfriendly.

Someone called from the house.

'Oh dear!' said Louisa. 'We'll have to go. D'you think he'll be all right?'

'Listen!' said Japhet, going close up and speaking loudly into the man's ear. 'You can stay here – d'you understand? We'll bring you some more to eat if we can. At any rate in the morning, if not tonight. But you will stay, won't you? Because we might have something very important to tell you!'

The man grunted; it was impossible to tell whether he understood or not. Then he turned away as if to go to sleep. So they left him.

'I say!' Louisa stopped dead as they got outside. 'You don't suppose he'll try to light a fire, do you? Because if he did, the whole place would go up in flames.'

'He hasn't got his frying-pan,' said Japhet in a final voice.

'I might try and take him a hot drink later on,' said Louisa.

'I don't think he needs a hot drink,' said Rose, 'so much as a hot *bath*! He absolutely stinks!'

'Ssh! He might hear!'

'Well, what d'you expect?' said Japhet. 'Tramps can't go about having baths. That's why they grow beards,' he added shortly.

'I suppose,' said Louisa, 'we could, possibly, get him some sort of washing arrangements. There's the outside tap. It'd mean carrying cans –'

'Washing!' said Rose. 'He needs more than just washing! He needs a thorough good scrub, all over!' She was echoing her mother. 'Whatever must he be like behind the ears?'

'It's mostly his feet,' Japhet remarked. 'They certainly do pong. Otherwise he's not too bad.'

'Well, *I* think he absolutely stinks,' said Rose.

'You said that before.'

'That means I mean it.'

'I say,' said Japhet. 'it would be rather good, though, wouldn't it, to let him have a real bath! I bet he'd love it! I bet he hasn't had one for ages. Couldn't we, one day when they're out –'

'We're *not* taking him into our bathroom,' Louisa interrupted firmly. 'Besides, what d'you mean, "one day"? How long d'you think he's going to stay?'

'Well, as long as he likes. If he *is* the Captain, he's got a perfect right to, you said so yourself.'

'Not a *perfect* right,' said Louisa. 'Just a – a *moral* right, that's all.'

'What's that?'

'I'm not sure, but it's certainly not perfect. It generally means you ought to be able to but you can't, if you get me.'

'I don't,' said Japhet. 'Anyway, we could give it to him out there.'

'What?'

'The bath.'

'What in?'

'Well, you did Oats in the old boiler thing, didn't you? – That used to be for making jam?'

'Ugh!' said Rose. 'I'll never eat jam again!'

'Don't be so silly,' Louisa scoffed, '*that* wasn't the jam thing at all, it was just an old dustbin that we've lost the lid of. But it wouldn't be any good for a person, it's much too small. Even Oats thought so, and he's only a medium-sized dog.'

'I know!' Japhet lit up. 'There's an actual old bath over in that gipsy place – I saw it, upside down in the bushes. We could get him that! Then he'd have a proper bathroom of his own!'

'How would the water run out?' Louisa asked.

'Through the plug-hole, what d'you think?'

'But where to? You couldn't just let it pour out all over the chicken house.'

'I might be able to dig a trench,' said Japhet thoughtfully, 'to take it under the side wall and out into those nettles. It'd get lost there all right.'

'I've got that duck soap,' volunteered Rose, 'that I had for my birthday. I used the Mickey Mouse and the bear, but there's a duck left; he can have that if he likes.'

'And there are some old towels in the kitchen cupboard.'

'Wait a minute!' said Louisa. 'Who d'you imagine is going to *get* this precious bath, anyway? It takes nearly ten minutes to walk to the gipsies' place *without* a bath. Who's going to carry it all that way?'

'We are,' said Japhet.

'Not likely! For one thing, I bet it's jolly heavy, and

for another thing, *I'm* not going to be seen carrying an old bath down the road in broad daylight! Suppose we met someone from school!'

'Yes!' said Rose fervently. 'Just suppose!'

Japhet looked at them. There was no doubt about it, when the shadow of that girls' school came between them, they were poles apart.

'All right,' he said, 'I'll have to get somebody else.'

Chapter Eighteen

And that was how Japhet and Derek came to be carrying an extremely rusty old bath across the common and over the road, early on Sunday morning.

Japhet had rushed round to Derek's, on Louisa's bike, the evening before. He had even missed the Black Riders, which showed how keen he was (though he did see the very end of it at Derek's; but he didn't tell Louisa this).

Derek, of course, took the thing up at once. You would have thought he had spent his whole life moving baths off commons, from the way he talked.

'Ease her over!' he called, as they negotiated the plank bridge where, in winter, a stream crossed the common.

'Steady on! Heel her round a bit! O.K.' – He carried on as if they were manoeuvring a ship or a complicated field-gun. To Japhet, the only thing that mattered was the weight – and whether the Captain would still be there.

He was. They could hear his snoring as they edged the bath, at last, round the elderberry tree on the way to the chicken house door. Japhet only prayed that his parents wouldn't hear it too.

'Ssh!' he hissed at Derek. 'Better leave her here! We can drag her inside later!'

Derek, for all his airs and orders, was not sorry to

put his end of the bath down. It was pretty heavy, and the curved-over rusted edge bit into the ends of your fingers. They had had to have several rests on the way across the common, though Derek behaved as if these were not 'rests' so much as pauses for the issuing of fresh orders.

'Thanks,' panted Japhet, sitting on the tap end. 'Would you like to see him? We can squint through a crack in the boards.' He offered this as if it were the highest possible reward for Derek's good turn. But Derek wasn't particularly interested in the tramp; the bath was another matter, partly because it meant getting something for nothing, and Derek always approved of that. He also liked the early morning, though he couldn't have said why. He didn't talk about things easily. During one of their pauses on the common, with the bath tilted between blackberry bushes, Japhet had looked at the dew and said 'I'd like to *drink* it, wouldn't you?' But Derek only grunted and said he'd rather have a coke. Japhet left it at that: he hadn't meant *really* drink it, of course; he sometimes thought even Derek was just a tiny bit dim. And now, not to see the interest of having a real tramp in the chicken house! Or course, Derek didn't know about the Captain, but you'd have thought even an ordinary tramp was quite interesting. But Derek seemed content simply to have moved the bath; just a technical operation – nothing to do with people at all.

Japhet couldn't resist having a squint through one of the cracks himself. But all he could see was a vague outline in the hay. The snoring went on, rhythmically.

'If only he knew,' grinned Japhet, 'what we've got

166

for him! Wouldn't he be pleased! – Here, we'd better drag it where it can't be seen from the house, in case anybody asks questions.'

So they heaved the bath through the nettles, and left it on the far side of the chicken house. Jo ambled up to inspect it.

'She probably thinks it's a new drinking-trough. By the way, would you like some milk?'

Derek said he wouldn't mind, which meant Yes; so they crept into the kitchen and took a bottle out of the fridge.

'Got any bread?' said Derek. Japhet found a loaf.

'Bacon?'

'They'd smell it upstairs,' Japhet protested.

'No, cold. On the bread. My dad always takes bread'n bacon –'

'What, raw?'

'Yeah.' Derek put on his backwoodsman's voice.

'All right, let's go and eat them on the common; we can have a picnic.' Anything to get Derek out of the house before the others came down. Japhet didn't think the raw bacon was nice at all, when he came to that; but he put up a fair show of eating it, and stuffed the fat deep in the grass when Derek wasn't looking.

'I wish you could be here for the actual bath.'

'You're not really going to make him get in?'

'He won't need making. When he hears all that water sploshing about, ready, and smells the soap, he'll be so glad he won't know what to say! He'll be *amazed*!' And Japhet lay back, regardless of the dew, and looked happily up at the clearing sky. It was going to be a fine day. Which meant, among other things, that there'd be no nonsense about putting up indoor clothes lines.

'Some job!' grunted Derek.

'What?'

'This bath idea. If I was you, I'd stick the plug in and leave it for a drinking-trough. Much better.'

'That reminds me,' said Japhet, 'I'll have to find a plug; there wasn't one. – I wonder if he'll look very different.'

'Who?'

'The Cap – I mean the tramp.'

'Oh. Well, don't blame me, that's all.'

'Blame you what for?'

'I dunno. Whatever happens.'

'What *can* happen? Anybody'd think a person had never had a bath before.'

'Well, pigs don't,' said Derek, 'and they're clean.' He got up to go. Japhet went back home, thinking how many watering-cans and bucketsful it would need to make a really decent bath. That time when all the water had been turned off, he remembered, it had seemed to take a lot of jugs to fill even a washbasin; but they were small jugs.

'Where's that bacon?' his mother was saying. 'I'm sure I had a couple of rashers left.'

'Oh!' said Japhet. Louisa looked at him, and immediately thought he must have taken it to the chicken-house.

'I don't want any,' she said hastily.

'You couldn't if you did,' her mother said, banging the fridge door. 'Really, sometimes I wonder if Oats can open this fridge, the way things – Japhet!' She suddenly saw his red face. 'And I was saving that for your father's Sunday breakfast!'

'Perhaps he'd like an egg,' said Louisa, going to fetch one. 'Or two, on toast. I'll do them.' Anything to get away from the subject of bacon.

'Where's the dirty frying-pan, then?' asked her mother. 'You don't mean to say you ate it *raw*!' She knew Japhet wouldn't have washed the pan.

'I did,' mumbled Japhet. Louisa thought he was telling a lie until she saw him actually slipping out of the larder with bread and cheese.

'He hasn't had anything yet,' he muttered. 'Snoring. It was Derek, the bacon. We've got it!' From these cryptic remarks Louisa concluded that the bath was ready.

'Well, not exactly ready,' said Japhet later, as they stood round the rusty object in the nettles. 'I've got to find a plug.'

Louisa thought she had seen a spare one in the mug on the kitchen mantelpiece; but it turned out to be much too small.

'We could put sticking-plaster round it,' said Rose.

'Silly, that'd wash off. What about plasticine?'

'That might do,' Louisa allowed. 'But we've got to get the bath inside first, and dig that trench.'

'That won't take long,' said Japhet cheerfully.

But he was too hopeful, as usual. The chicken-house floor was trodden down as hard as brick; hacking away with the corner of a spade, it took Japhet an hour to make a thing that Louisa said was more like a scratch than a trench.

'I know!' said Japhet. 'We'll siphon it out with the

hose pipe!'

'What, the whole hose?' Louisa didn't much like this idea; the hose was goodness knows how long, and it always took their father about half an hour to get it back on the iron wheel thing where it was kept; and even then it generally got twisted and tangled, with odd loops hanging out. Louisa always wondered why nothing like that was ever quite right in their house; so different from the TV advertisements, where people in absolutely holeless pullovers wound up hoses slickly and symmetrically, or brought out of shining ovens scones that were all the same size and shape. . . .

'Perhaps we needn't,' said Japhet, remembering that last time he had got the hose out there had been some trouble, and a lot of talk about never doing it again.

'– Or *I* know!' he said, brightening. 'We could cut a piece off – just a little short piece – and fasten it to the outside of the bath where the water runs out, and push the other end out through one of the cracks between the boards of the chicken house!'

'Cut a piece off the hose?' said Rose, sounding shocked.

'Only a titchy bit, silly, they'd never notice. Then we should have our own drain!' Before Louisa could stop him, he had rushed off to get a sharp knife.

'Well,' she said to Rose, 'you'd better fetch your plasticine. It's all very well to get the water to run out, but first it's got to be made to stay in.'

'What colour?' asked Rose.

'Good heavens, any.' Really, that bath ought to be cleaned, Louisa said to herself as Rose went off. If this thing were to be done at all, it must be done properly and thoroughly. So she went to get the Vim and a rag.

'What d'you want it for?' her mother asked casually.

'Oh, nothing. Just to clean something up.'

As it was Sunday morning, the kitchen was in the usual shambles of pastry-making and left-over breakfast things and their father with the vacuum-cleaner upside down, mending it, and a saucepan of cocoa boiling over for his elevenses – so that with all this, their mother asked no more questions and was only too glad the children were keeping out of the way.

The tramp, to their surprise, slept on until well after ten o'clock.

'Poor thing,' said Louisa, 'he must have been tired.'

Japhet arranged the bread and cheese neatly on a tin plate for him to find when he did wake; Louisa covered it over with a clean handkerchief to keep off the flies. Rose picked an egg-cupful of raspberries from the vegetable garden, and insisted on putting them there too. He would be glad of them, she said.

Meanwhile, Louisa got some of the dirt off the bath, and helped Japhet to drag it inside the chicken-house.

It was then that the man woke up, grunted, muttered and began to scratch himself.

'Good morning,' said Louisa.

'It's the hay,' Japhet said, 'there are little things in it. I always get bitten when I lie in any hay. They go off, though.'

'Specially if you have a *bath*,' Louisa said pointedly.

'There's some breakfast there,' said Japhet, pushing the tin plate under the man's hand. The man still sat scratching; he looked dazed.

171

'He's not properly awake yet,' Louisa murmured, 'leave him alone for a bit.'

'I picked those,' said Rose, as she saw his hand on the egg-cup. 'Would you like some sugar on them? I *could* get a bit of top-of-the-milk –'

But he interrupted her, For the second time, he said in a clear voice one downright word:

'Tea.'

They looked at each other. He looked between them, into space.

'Drop o' tea,' he said again, flatly, as if he were stating a fact.

'He might say "please",' whispered Rose. But Louisa had decided that the poor old man certainly was a bit batty, whatever or whoever else he might be.

'We understand,' she said kindly and slowly. 'I'll try and get you a cup of tea. You just wait here.'

'Do you like China or Indian?' said Rose.

'Don't be so dim!' Japhet told her.

'Well, that's what people do say.' She had heard her mother ask it, so it must be right. It was not fair of Japhet to be so squashing.

Louisa managed to make the tea without exciting any comment from her mother; but this time, instead of putting a tea-pot and milk jug and sugar basin, as for Mr Cuthbertson, she filled one very large mug – an old one that they sometimes used for painting-water. It was a bit stained inside; those poster-paints were hard to get off – but he wouldn't see that, and she was sure it wouldn't taste. And she knew it wasn't true about green paint being poisonous. She knew, too, that all tramps and people like that took sugar, so she put in three spoonfuls, and on second thoughts took the packet with her too. She even remembered a spoon – but being a cautious and level-headed girl, she didn't take one of the better ones (none could be called 'best').

'I've told him!' said Japhet when she got back to the chicken-house. 'I made him feel all round the bath, and he knows where the towel is, and Rose has gone to get that duck. I've even made a bath mat!' he added with great pride. He pointed to a piece of sacking laid neatly on the floor, with the remains of an old door-mat placed in the middle of it.

'That'll be awfully scratchy,' said Rose, coming in. 'And what if he gets out the other side?'

'He knows which is his left and right, doesn't he?' said Japhet crossly. No-one seemed to appreciate his efforts.

Louisa looked at the man sitting on the hay.

'I don't think you should have broken it to him yet,' she said in a low voice. 'Not before he's had his tea.' The man was muttering to himself; he didn't look very happy.

'Here you are; and there's the sugar, in case you want some more.' She put the mug and the packet into his hands; to all their astonishment, when he had tasted the tea he carefully emptied the whole of the rest of the packet into the mug. Then he stirred vigorously with the old spoon, and drank it with relish, smacking his lips from time to time and wiping his mouth on his hay-fringed cuff.

All that sugar! thought Louisa. It was most unfair that some people never got fat. But then, she relented, perhaps he hadn't been having enough to eat for ages.

Certainly everything they had given him had gone – even that old bright yellow jam tart that Japhet had snatched at the last minute from the pantry shelf, where it had been for at least a fortnight.

And could this possibly be Captain Noah, this poor, hungry, muttering scarecrow of a man? She saw the tattoo marks as he stretched out his arm to pat Oats, who by now had decided that this was a friend. Again the man spoke clearly.

'Doggie!' he said. 'That's right. Doggie!'

'Do you like dogs?' Japhet asked.

'*He* had a bath yesterday,' said Rose encouragingly. The man stared in their direction.

'Had a dog once,' he said. 'Black. Ah.' And he fell to muttering again.

'What was his name?' said Japhet.

'You *should* have a dog, being blind,' Rose said, staring at him. 'But not Oats, he's ours.'

'Black,' said the man, and patted Oats's head.

'I suppose he died?' said Rose, who always liked to hear about disasters.

But the man was silent; he didn't seem to have heard. Japhet decided to be bold.

'Did he fall down a well?' he said. Still no answer. 'Listen,' Japhet whispered to Louisa, 'it *must* be him: what with the boot and that ship mark on his arm *and* the dog –'

'Lots of people have dogs,' said Louisa.

'But when I said about the well, he didn't say No. Why don't you *ask* him? We've got to, some time.'

'All right, I will.' Louisa took a deep breath. She raised her voice 'I say,' she said, 'are you by any chance

174

called Noah?'

They waited, their eyes fixed on him intently.

'I don't believe he heard,' said Japhet.

'He must of,' said Rose; 'She absolutely shouted.'

'Ask him again.'

Louisa went up and tapped the man on the shoulder. 'We know somebody,' she said loudly and carefully, 'called Noah. At least, we know *of* him. And we think it might be you.'

'Now you've made him suspicious,' said Japhet. 'Probably thinks we're going to set the police after him or something.' The man was scratching his head and looking worried.

'What is your name?' said Louisa more gently. A different expression came over the man's face – a knowing glint. And quite clearly he said:

'All sorts!'

'Allsorts?' said Rose. 'That's liquorice.'

'No, he means he's got more than one, I expect. We've got two names each,' Louisa went on, trying to sound friendly and reassuring. 'But a girl at school had four.'

'Who?' interrupted Japhet suspiciously.

'Jane Fergusson, if you must know. She's lucky, she'll have more to choose from when she grows up. Have *you* got a lot to choose from?' she asked the man.

'He was a black dog,' he said.

They looked at each other in despair. Japhet, behind the man's back, touched his forehead with his finger, and Louisa nodded. It was worse than she had thought.

'I don't see how we're to find out anything, at this

rate,' she said when they got outside again.

'But look at all the clues!' protested Japhet. 'Everything goes to show he's Noah, but he probably doesn't want to say so yet.'

'It may be all just coincidence,' Louisa warned. But Japhet wasn't going to have the glory of his discovery overcast by any doubts.

'Perhaps he'll tell us when he's clean,' he said. 'It may make all the difference. Anyway, I'm sure he *is* Noah. I'm certain!'

'And I'm not,' said Louisa.

'Anyway,' said Rose, 'he still does need a bath.'

Chapter Nineteen

Hot water was the main difficulty. Everything else was all set – blue and yellow plasticine pressed round the plug, a piece of hose-pipe pushed under the chicken-house wall, the duck soap laid ready on a toffee-tin lid, an old bath towel hanging on a string between two nails.

'I know,' said Japhet, going back to his hose idea, 'couldn't we fix one end of the hose to the hot tap in the kitchen, and out through the window – it'd easily reach to here!'

'No,' said Louisa.

'Well, we could light a fire in the field, out of sight, and fill that dustbin, and –'

'No,' said Louisa even more positively.

'Of course, it'd take some time. But after all, he doesn't want it boiling.'

'Perhaps he'd like a *cold* bath,' Rose suggested. 'But I suppose it wouldn't get him really clean.'

'He wouldn't like it, either,' said Louisa, 'nobody really does.'

'Derek has cold baths,' Japhet said, 'he told me so.'

'I bet he lets some hot in.' Louisa didn't trust Derek. 'Anyway,' she went on before there could be an argument, 'we'll just have to boil up some kettles and saucepans and rush out with them as quickly as possible. We can have some cold water ready to mix in.'

'Oughtn't he to have clean clothes?' said Rose. 'It's not very nice to have a bath and then put on all dirty things.'

'Well, I'm not washing *his*, and that's that,' Louisa said.

Then Japhet remembered that there were some old things of their father's in the spare-room wardrobe. He rushed off and fetched a pair of grey trousers, quite all right except for some splashes of white paint; a jacket, a grey shirt that had had a new tail (bright green; but their mother did her best), a pair of odd socks, a straw hat and a very gaudy tie.

'Oh!' said Rose, taking this up, 'how lovely! Where did you get it?'

'It's one Aunt Freda sent for Christmas,' said Louisa; she recognised it as the sort that her father always put away at once. It had orange foxes on a purple ground.

'What a pity he won't be able to see it,' Rose said; she was sorry to have to part with the tie.

They took the things into the chicken-house and laid them out neatly over a sack of potatoes. Then they showed the man where they were; he picked up each garment and felt it all over; he seemed to approve – at any rate, he put the hat on straight away, perched like a biscuit on his thick white curls.

'He'd look funny bathing in that,' giggled Japhet.

'They're for when you've had your bath,' said Rose clearly.

The man stood stock still. 'Eh?' he said sharply.

'I told you, we're going to give you a nice hot bath,' said Japhet. 'In a minute.'

'Well, half an hour,' said Louisa. The man drew

back. 'Not *give* it you,' Louisa explained, 'just put it ready. We shan't be in here, of course!'

'It *is* ready,' said Japhet, 'except for the water.'

'Just come and sit down, and we'll tell you when.' Louisa guided him back to the hay.

'Drop o' tea?' he said.

'Oh dear, not tea *again*!' Louisa murmured in some dismay. They'd never get the bath filled, at this rate. She had a momentary suspicion that the man was trying to put it off.

'Sorry we haven't got any rum, Captain,' Japhet said in a hearty voice. The man made no response. 'Captain Fogwill, I *should* say,' Japhet repeated more loudly. 'Or is it Frogwell? We weren't sure.'

'Tea,' said the figure in the hay. Japhet shrugged, and pulled a face at Louisa. All right, so his bold shot in the dark hadn't come off – but he'd do better next time. He'd prove his point.

Meanwhile, there was all the water to be heated. They knew that on Sunday afternoon their mother and father would be reading or gardening; the kitchen would be empty. This was the time to do it.

Louisa made a mug of tea with the new instant tea-mix stuff. Then she filled saucepans from the hot tap, to make things quicker. As soon as Japhet had taken one through the open window, emptied it and brought it back, on it went again. Louisa had the four gas burners going full blast; altogether she had heated up fourteen saucepanfuls and four kettlefuls when she heard her mother coming in from the garden.

'That'll have to be enough!' she said quickly to Japhet. 'Where's Rose?'

'I've put her in charge of the cold. She's got the watering-can.'

'Well, that's the last of the hot, quick!' She handed him the saucepan, just as her mother came in and said cheerfully, 'Hallo – doing some washing?'

'In a way.' Louisa was too truthful to make up some story; she just hoped there would be no more questions.

'Where's Japhet going with that saucepan?'

'Only to the chicken-house.'

'It's my best one.'

'I know; I'll see he brings it back.'

'Well, mind you do. Would you like to go and cut a lettuce for tea?' Her mother gave her the old knife with the burnt handle, and Louisa gladly escaped and went straight to the chicken-house.

Japhet and Rose were standing outside.

'There's a bit of extra cold in the can – d'you want it?' Japhet called through a crack. No answer.

'You'd better come,' Louisa said, 'or they'll be wondering. And bring that saucepan. Is he all right?'

'I should jolly well hope so,' said Japhet. 'Are you all right?' he called. Silence. 'Anyway, we've made it absolutely smashing, haven't we, Rose? I even put a flannel!'

'Whose? What colour?'

'Green, I think.'

'That's mine!' said Louisa indignantly. Really, there was a limit.

'Well, he needs it more,' said Japhet.

'Thanks for the compliment,' said Louisa.

'I can't hear any splashing.' Rose had her ear to the door.

'Are you sure he knows where everything is?' Louisa asked.

'I showed him three times,' Japhet said.

'I suppose it's too late,' Rose wondered, 'to give him a bath salt? I've still got one I had off the Christmas tree.'

'It's too late,' Louisa told her. Their mother was calling from the house. 'Anyway,' she said, 'he might not even like it. The bath itself'll be enough, without anything thrown in.'

'Still, I expect he'll feel better when he's had it,' Japhet said comfortably. 'He might even talk better, you never know.'

'Baths are supposed to loosen people up,' Louisa agreed.

'Yes, I bet he'll come out feeling fresh as a daisy!' Japhet beamed. 'Good old Noah – hope he doesn't have a flood! – And then when he's all scrubbed and bright, we can tell him the good news. Those papers in the airing-cupboard *must* be dry by now.'

'Well, we'll see about that,' said Louisa carefully. 'There's no need to rush. What did he say while you were pouring in the water?'

'Nothing.'

'What did he do?'

'Nothing. Just sat.'

'Did he seem excited?'

'He scratched a bit.'

'Well, pleased, then?'

'No,' said Rose, who was as truthful as her sister. 'I didn't think he looked at all pleased.'

'But he will be!' said Japhet. 'You wait!'

'I thought,' Rose said slowly, 'he looked rather as if –'

But no-one heard 'as if' what; their mother was ringing the cow-bell energetically, and their father was calling from the garden; they had to go. Rose was always being left with half-finished sentences.

'Japhet, you haven't finished your milk!' their mother said at tea-time. 'Whatever's the matter with you all today? Louisa, don't you want some cake? Rose, another tomato?'

They were all, of course, aching to get back to the chicken-house.

'I want to see how that drain works,' Japhet muttered to Louisa.

'D'you think he'll have used all the soap?' Rose whispered. 'Actually, he can keep what's left.'

'A lot of mumbling going on,' their father remarked. 'Can't we all hear?'

At last tea was over.

'Can I get down?' asked Rose. Louisa saw a piece of lettuce sticking out of her pocket.

'He won't eat that!' she whispered.

'Why not? I thought it'd be nice and cool, after the –'

'Ssh! Come on,' said Louisa hastily.

'What's the great game?' their father asked when they had all rushed off.

'Oh, I don't know. Something in the chicken-house. I expect they're pretending to camp there. Trust Japhet.'

'I don't,' said their father, 'that's just it.'

'Oh, they're all right,' said their mother, 'Louisa's with them.'

'I thought I saw Japhet mucking about with that hose,' said their father, and went out looking doubtful.

Meanwhile, Japhet had arrived at the chicken-house door. He knocked.

'Can I come in now?'

The girls hurried up behind him.

'Ask him if he's ready to have the water let out,' said Louisa. Japhet asked.

'Say Is he dry.' It seemed proper, somehow, for the man of the party to be talking to the bather inside.

'Did you find the towel all right?' Japhet called.

'I hope he hasn't drowned,' said Rose. '– Well, you *can* drown in a bath.'

'I know, but you needn't be so cheerful,' said Louisa irritably. She herself was alarmed at the complete silence inside there.

Not a splash, not a drip, not the slightest shuffle of anybody dressing; not so much as a rustle of hay.

'Perhaps he's gone to sleep again,' she said. 'Look through the crack.'

Japhet looked. Louisa, gazing at the fair tuft on the back of his head, thought she saw even that change colour.

'I say!' he gasped. 'Well, of all the –!' He flung open the door.

They gathered together in the entrance, then walked slowly in.

'Oh *no*!' said Louisa. But she saw at once that it was really Oh Yes. 'When? How? He can't have! We should have seen him!'

The bath was full.

The chicken-house was empty.

Rose picked up the untouched duck. Japhet looked at the greenish water, with the rust showing clearly through.

'He never even got *in*!' he said, outraged. 'The un-grateful old –'

'He's taken the clothes,' Louisa interrupted. 'And our mug. And that tin plate.'

'I thought he would,' said Rose. The others turned on her.

'Miss Clever, aren't you!' snapped Japhet.

'Why, what d'you mean?' Louisa said suspiciously. Perhaps the man had said something, and Rose hadn't told them? But no, Rose had merely watched and thought.

'The more we got the bath ready,' she said, 'the more he didn't look pleased. I suppose he just likes dirt best. That's all.'

Louisa sat down on the edge of the unused bath. With a pang she realised that they had been so much taken up with their own ideas about getting it ready, and how to arrange it, that they had hardly given a thought to the man who was actually to have it! And there he had sat, blindly listening to the preparations, too dumb-founded perhaps, to protest – except by the one simple, drastic step of going away.

'And now,' Louisa lamented bitterly, 'we shall never know if it was the Captain or not! Our last chance gone!'

'He might come back,' Japhet said, but doubtfully.

'Never,' said Louisa. 'I'm sure we've scared him off for good.'

'Well, perhaps it wasn't him after all,' said Japhet, changing his whole point of view in order to look on the bright side. 'And in that case, it doesn't matter.'

'I liked that mug!' said Rose. 'It was a useful mug.'

184

'The awful thing is, we shall never *know*,' Louisa repeated. 'We shall never be sure. Suppose it *was* him, and we just did the one thing to send him away!'

'I could go and look in the gipsy place again,' Japhet suggested.

'He'd never come back now,' Louisa said, 'he wouldn't trust us.'

'Oh well,' said Japhet, 'anyone want a cold bath?'

'I'd like that plasticine back,' said Rose.

'All right, come on, let's see how the drain works –' – but Japhet was cut short by a loud shout from the distance. It was his father's voice, and it sounded very angry.

'Goodness, what's the matter now?' said Louisa.

They found their father standing in the middle of the lawn with an end of hose-pipe in each hand.

'Who,' he said, 'did this?' It seemed that the whole length of the hose had been neatly cut in half.

Everyone looked at Japhet.

'Well, I only wanted a *bit*,' he said, 'and I couldn't find the ends, they were all tucked in somewhere, so I just cut off one of the loops.'

'A *loop*!' said Louisa.

'You shouldn't of,' Rose said disapprovingly.

'Cut off a *loop*!' shouted their father. 'Of all the blithering, half-witted, fat-headed, crack-brained, daft – Japhet, you coot! You donkey! You – you –'

'Clot,' supplied Rose, only wanting to help. It didn't mean she was *against* Japhet, though he looked at her as if it did.

'But what did you *do* it for, you ass?' said their father. 'I can't understand anybody, even you, being such a complete and utter beetle-brained goose, such a beef-witted cuckoo, as to. . . .' And so he went on.

Mixed metaphors, thought Louisa, who had just done them at school.

More trouble, thought Japhet.

It *is* a pity about that mug, thought Rose.

None of them, at that moment, thought about the search for the Captain, or of how it would end – if it had not already ended.

But however angry people are, there's always a next day.

Chapter Twenty

To begin with, the policeman called again – though they were all at school, and didn't know till afterwards.

'They've found that gipsy!' their mother told them at tea. 'Somewhere in Sussex. And he owned up.'

'Have you got the ring?' Japhet asked. Their mother hesitated, and Louisa noticed her go a faint pink that clashed with her pale orange cotton frock.

'Well, yes,' she said, 'as a matter of fact I have. I found it this morning.'

'*Found* it?' Louisa sat up and looked her straight in the eye; her mother grinned shamefacedly.

'It was in the ironing drawer all the time,' she said. 'Underneath all those bills, and Oats's old collar, and that cake frill off Rose's last birthday –'

'I *told* you you ought to tidy that drawer!' Louisa broke in. 'Really, this house!' – But of course, she wouldn't have changed it – not for Georgia's panelled billiard-room; not for all the Carters' bright horse-brasses and dull brocade.

'Tidy it yourself, then,' said Japhet to Louisa; he sometimes felt his mother needed support. 'Whatever did the policeman say, though?'

'I do keep the actual iron there,' their mother said meekly. '– And he just said good, he was glad I'd found it. He was very nice. Of course, it was the one place I hadn't looked.'

'But what about the study?' asked Japhet. 'You said the gipsy owned up –'

'Yes, he did. It seems one of the boys had told him some silly story about our having something hidden, something valuable – he didn't even seem to know what. And he's a bit, well, queer, according to the police, and he had some vague idea of "paying us out," so he kept telling them –'

'What for?' Japhet said quickly.

'I really don't know. He *was* annoyed about the pony, but that was some time before – it all seems such a muddle. All I could gather was that he thought he might find something, but even if he didn't, he wanted to be a nuisance.'

'Nuisance!' gasped Louisa.

'Well, I think perhaps he *is* a bit odd,' said her mother; 'the police seem to think so too.' Louisa reflected that there seemed to be a number of odd people around – though of course some of them were nicely so, like Mr Cuthbertson.

'Have they arrested him?' Japhet asked.

'No. I think we shall drop the whole thing.'

'Can you do that?' said Louisa. 'I thought people who broke in *had* to be prosecuted.'

'Apparently not. If we don't want to charge him, the police may just let it go. And I don't think we do. It's not as if he actually took anything after all.'

'But he intended to,' said Louisa.

'We'd have to prove that.'

'It's pretty obvious. People don't go breaking into

people's houses just for fun.'

'They might,' said Japhet, who could imagine it.

'He seems to have had *some* idea at the back of his mind,' their mother said, 'but it all looks rather amateurish. And although he's not a very nice man, I didn't take to him myself, at least he's never been in court. And there are those children to think of – suppose he went to prison, what would happen to them?

'Yes, I quite liked Danny,' said Louisa, 'and you can't really blame him for sticking up for his family. I suppose I'd stick up for you, however horrible you were.'

'Thank you,' said their mother.

'Was it actually *in* the cake-frill?' asked Rose.

The importance of all this had made their mother forget to tell Louisa that there was a letter for her in the hall. It had come by the second post.

'Might it be a biscuit?' said Louisa. 'You know I sent for that free sample. Four labels.'

'Call that free?' said Japhet.

'Why can't *I* have a biscuit – it's not fair –' began Rose.

'*Dog* biscuit!' said Louisa. 'To give Oats more vitamins.'

'He has quite enough,' their mother said. 'We don't want him getting any *worse*.'

But the letter was too thin to contain so much as a wafer. And the envelope was typed, with a local postmark.

'Who on *earth*? . . .' said Louisa, and tore it open. For a moment she thought it might be some joke of Georgia's.

When she had read it, she sat down bang on the stairs.

She read it again, then called Japhet, in such an odd voice that Rose came running too.

'It's from – it's from –'

'Who?' Japhet snatched the letter out of her hand, and she was too weak even to hold on to it.

'Coo!' he said. '*Coo!*'

'What person is that?' asked Rose.

'Don't be dim – it's from Mr Glover!'

'The museum one,' Louisa said. 'that Japhet saw, and that I wrote to –'

'*Who* you wrote to,' said Rose, to get her own back for once. But Louisa was much too much excited to notice. She grabbed back the letter.

'What does he say, what does he say?' asked Japhet.

'He says he's been busy, and not well, or he would have – oh, etcetera, etcetera,' said Louisa impatiently; 'but listen to this: he says perhaps the person we mean is a Mr *Noel* Fogwill, who did live here, at this address, but who moved when the house was sold – *moved*, mind you! "And is now, as far as I know, living with a sister at Bognor Regis. The last address he wrote from was" – and then there's an address. And then it says "P.S. I have no information as to size of boots. You would have to ask him personally." *Well!*' Louisa lay back on the stairs for a minute, limp.

'But it's not the right name,' said Japhet. Noah was a good name; at least, it made his own seem better; he didn't want to give it up.

Louisa pulled herself together.

'Noel and Noah could sound alike,' she said. 'The Gillingses might have got it wrong. I'm going to find out.' She was sitting bolt upright now. Suddenly she felt this was the last great opportunity, the final effort that absolutely must be made to clear the whole thing up. And just when she had thought it was all over! But the letter from Mr Glover made it real in a new way; a more grown-up way; a way that could be followed up, surely, with the kind of reasonableness that would be comforting after all these fires and wells and burglaries and tramps and baths. . . .

'What place does he say?' asked Japhet.

'Bognor Regis. That's on the south coast. Sussex.'

'That's where the gipsy was,' Rose pointed out. 'They might be together, or next door.'

'Gipsies don't have doors,' said Japhet.

'They do; caravan ones.'

'Anyway, Sussex is huge,' said Louisa, 'so it's not likely we should run into the gipsy.'

'But suppose we write to this Noel chap,' said Japhet, 'and he *is* blind, and the sister's wicked and doesn't let him see the letter, but makes him sign something and then gets all the money for herself –' Japhet's imagination was running riot.

'Really, you are hopeless,' said Louisa. 'Why *should* the sister be wicked? Bognor's a very respectable place. Besides, if the Gillingses were wrong about his name, they may be wrong about other things too; perhaps he's not blind at all. Mr Glover doesn't say so. And anyway,' she wound up, her eyes going a little brighter as she sat solidly on the third stair, 'I shan't write to him!'

'What will you do, then?'

'I shall go!'

'Where?' asked Rose blankly.

'To Bognor.'

'When?' said Japhet.

'As soon as possible.'

'But *how*?' he persisted. 'However can you?'

'I don't know. I haven't thought. But I will. I'll find a way, somehow. I tell you, I just absolutely *will*!'

And Rose and Japhet knew she would.

They even made way for her, respectfully, as she walked upstairs.

Chapter Twenty-one

'Now, young friends,' said the old gentleman, seeming to look at them acutely, with his head cocked on one side. 'What can I do for you?'

'Perhaps they'd like a bulls-eye,' said the lady. She had a nose just the same shape as the old gentleman's, long and narrow with a bit tilted up at the end.

'Anybody vote for bulls-eyes?' the old gentleman asked.

'Thank you,' said Louisa.

'Some of us do,' said Japhet.

Rose said nothing, but took one when it came.

They were all three packed together on a shiny pink chintz sofa in the front room of Number Forty, Tamarisk Terrace, Bognor Regis. How had they got there? Well, you will guess that it was Louisa's doing; but we shall hear more about that later. Meanwhile, opposite them, on a chair to match, sat the old gentleman, wearing steel-rimmed spectacles and a very thick white pullover with a knobbly pattern knitted into the front. His sister, in identical spectacles, sat on a straight chair by the window when she had given out the bulls-eyes. She picked up some knitting; it looked like another thick pullover, exactly the same as the one he was wearing, but navy blue.

The room was small and shiny; the empty brass coal-scuttle shone; the gold-framed pictures shone; the table and straight-backed chairs were polished, black as negroes; the apples shone in a glass dish on the sideboard; there was a firescreen like a galleon and made of gleaming copper.

Yet it was cosy, too, not cold as some over-polished rooms can be. Louisa noticed a jar of sweet-peas on the table; Japhet spotted a half-finished model ship stuck up in a corner, and some tattered magazines with pictures of yachts; Rose was immediately struck by the huge grey cat who lay in the middle of the rug. There was a photograph of him, too, stuck behind a tobacco tin on the mantelpiece.

'Well, now?' said the old gentleman. 'Tuck your bulls-eyes to starboard and go ahead!'

'First,' said Louisa, 'is it actually Frogwell or Fogwill?'

'And Noah or Noel?' said Japhet.

'Frogwill, Noel Horatio, late of His Majesty's Merchant Navy.'

'*Her* Majesty,' said Rose. 'The Queen's a Her.'

'Ah, but this was George Five, mate.'

'Horatio George, but that was the uncle's name!' Louisa exclaimed.

'Horatio George, him of Wagga Wagga – oh don't you talk to me about him, the silly old –'

'Now, Noel, not in front of the children, *please*!' His sister wagged her finger at him. 'You mustn't encourage him to get on to Uncle H.,' she said, 'it makes his blood pressure go high and his language go low!' She smiled at Louisa, with a dry twinkle, Louisa suspected that this sister of the Captain's was rather bright, even if she was at least seventy.

'But what brings you here?' said the Captain. It certainly was the Captain, this time – though how unlike the picture of him, and in what different surroundings!

'We live in your house,' said Louisa, thinking it best to be simple.

'The one you were turned out of,' added Japhet.

'We've got a boot of yours,' Rose said.

'Wait a minute, one at a time – what, that old place?' said the Captain in amazement. 'I should have thought they'd have pulled that down years ago! Whatever would you want to go and live there for?'

'But – but it was your *home*!' said Louisa.

'We think it was awful of him to put you out like that,' said Japhet.

'We've been trying to find you –'

'To rescue you –'

'To restore your rights,' Louisa said firmly.

'We nearly got the wrong person, but he went away.'

'He was only a tramp – I'm sorry,' said Louisa, embarrassed, 'but we didn't know what you'd be like.'

'We gave him a bath,' said Rose, 'at least, we would of.'

'And we found your papers, and your compass!' Japhet burst out, 'on the day the ceiling fell down – at least, some then and some later –'

'Steady, steady, steady!' The Captain interrupted, looking dazed, and waving his pipe at them. 'What in blazes is all this here about?' His sister looked at him warningly. 'Now then,' she said. Then she smiled at Louisa, and said 'Do tell us. It sounds most interesting.'

So Louisa told the whole story, and all about the papers and the money, and how she had been to Somerset House to see if he were dead – at this the Captain lay back in his chair and laughed until he had to wipe tears off the insides of his spectacles. That, he said, was really rich; he might be rising eighty but he was still going strong, and would do for many a year!

But his sister smiled kindly at Louisa, and said she thought it was a very sensible and good thing to have done; she was sure not many people would have taken so much trouble.

'And then to come all the way here – and all because they wanted you to have Uncle H's money,' she told her brother. She was not going to have them thinking they were being laughed at.

'His money!' snorted the Captain. 'You can tell *that* to the Marines!'

'Here are the papers,' said Louisa handing them over. 'They got wet but we dried them, that's why they look so wavy.'

'By thunder, me duplicates!' said the Captain. 'Wherever did you rout these out of?'

'Same place as this; the ceiling,' said Japhet, and produced the compass, which he had been nursing on his knee, done up in brown paper.

'Well, shakes alive! said the Captain. 'Fancy them landing that old thing!' He held it towards his sister; she took it, looked at it, and went on knitting. 'It was father's,' she said, 'wasn't it?'

'That's right; but the papers, I must have stuffed 'em up a crack when we had that ceiling plastered over. Or rather when Glover did. Then I forgot all about 'em!

Of course, I'd got the other set. Though I might as well have stuffed that lot up the same hole, for all the good it did me.'

'He did expect to have something from his uncle,' the sister explained, 'but when he went up to claim it –'

'You mean you *have* claimed it!' Japhet looked bitterly disappointed.

'Call it a claim!' said the Captain indignantly. 'All we got was a string of debts! What the dickens he was doing out there in Wagga Wagga all that time, beats me. And there was I, thinking along the lines of a few thousand head of cattle, to say the least –'

'And I said it served him right,' smiled the sister, 'for being so calculating.'

'Calculating!' exploded the Captain. 'Hear that? Wouldn't *you* do a bit of calculating' – he seemed to be addressing Japhet – 'if you had an uncle, unmarried, who'd been said to have a few millions he didn't know what to do with? And you the only surviving male? Wouldn't *you* give it a second thought?'

'Yes,' said Japhet, 'I would.'

'But who said he had millions?' asked Louisa.

'Just family gossip,' said the sister. 'I told him he should never have trusted it.'

'Well, they'd been saying it for years, ever since I could remember. "Wait till old Uncle Horatio goes," they used to say – I was brought up on those words, it was like a magic charm. "Wait till Uncle Horatio goes" – but they all dropped off themselves. I'm referring to me brothers,' he added, 'Charlie and Archie and all that lot. *She* never cared either way –' cocking his thumb towards his sister – 'but then, she's got her pension, plus the Post Office Savings, which I never went in for.'

'I was a teacher,' explained the sister. 'I once taught in the village school.'

'*My* school?' said Japhet.

'Oh, do you go there? Have they still got the belfry, and that clock?'

'Yes, but it's generally ten minutes fast.'

'It always was. I'm glad it's still the same.'

'Mind you,' said the Captain to Louisa, 'it all goes to show you can't believe what people say, she's right there.

'Some people,' his sister retorted, 'live in glass houses.' And she gave Louisa a definite wink. 'Anyway,' she added, 'you did have uncle's stamp album.'

'Stamp album!' said the Captain contemptuously. 'If he'd spent more time on his farm, and less licking bits of paper, we might be better off – not but what we aren't quite comfortable,' he went on. 'Look at this' – he rapped the wall – 'there's a decent job for you. Sound timbers. Damp-course. Cavity walls. Roof water-tight. Pipes lagged. Plaster smooth as a baby's bottom – none of those rotten old beams poking out all the time.'

'But we like them!' said Louisa. 'We thought you did too. What about the way you were turned out?'

'Onto the common,' said Rose.

'When it was your own old home,' Japhet put in.

'– And nowhere to go. We thought it was dreadful of Mr Glover; we were quite ashamed to be living there.'

The Captain looked towards his sister; she raised her eyebrows and gazed wonderingly at Louisa.

'Who's been telling you all this?' he asked. 'Who's been yarning?'

'Why, the Gillingses.'

'– Who used to live there too,' explained Rose.

'Mrs Gillings sent Mr Gillings to ask you to breakfast,' said Japhet, 'but you'd gone.'

'And she'd kept a brown egg,' said Rose.

'Oh, the *Gillingses*!' said the Captain. He lay back in his chair and sucked at his empty pipe; a wicked twinkle seemed to come into his eye. 'So *they* told you all this, did they?'

'Poor Gillingses – he teased them terribly,' said his sister.

'Well, they asked for it. Always wanting to study a person's private affairs. I never knew it had come off so well, though.'

'Now, Noel, they were very kind; they meant well,' his sister reproved him.

'She'd say that about the bosun when the ship went down,' grinned the Captain, ' "He meant well"!'

'All the same, they were good people, and you did lead them up the garden path.'

'Reckon I hadn't got much else to do, living in that dump. It was a kind of hobby,' he said.

'But didn't you *like* it there?' asked Louisa in astonishment. 'They said you were terribly upset about going.'

'They said you pointed a gun at Mr Glover!' Japhet really hoped this was true. The Captain lay back again and laughed until he had to dab his eyes.

'All nonsense,' said the sister. 'And it was very naughty of him. He and Mr Glover were always perfectly good friends.'

'Ah, that was a real lark!' said the Captain, still shaking. 'Gave 'em something to talk about in the long dark evenings, that did! – Well, you know these old country people, who've never been more than ten miles from home; you know how they get. Pick up a bit of gossip and chew it over till it's a different shape altogether. That was the way it was with the Gillingses. I suppose it all comes of not seeing the world,' he added more tolerantly.

'They were very kind,' said his sister. 'I don't think you should have teased them so – and for them to be thinking of it, after all these years!' She sounded severe, but Louisa saw her half-smiling.

'I believe it was them calling me Noah that set it off,' said the Captain. 'That tickled me, for a start. They never did get it right. Reckon they'd never heard of the name of Noel, anyway.'

'That wasn't their fault,' said his sister.

'No, but as soon as they started getting hold of the wrong end of the stick about Glover, that was more than I could resist. To tell the truth, I was a bit annoyed she'd found out about me cutting out the pieces from the papers –'

'Why did you cut out so many?' Louisa asked. 'You only needed the one.'

'Poking about my rooms,' the Captain went on, ignoring the question.

'Now, Noel, that's too bad! You know she was tidying up the house for you, out of sheer kindness.'

'All right, all right, but don't tell me she didn't keep her eyes skinned! Anyway, when I saw which way the wind was blowing, I thought I might as well fan it up a bit. Give 'em something worth talking about. So I started laying it on good and thick.'

'Including the language,' remarked his sister.

'Well, do 'em good. Bring a breath of sea air into their lives. A bit of salt. I was sorry for 'em, that was really it. Besides, I'd ease off when I thought the old lady was really beginning to heel over. They enjoyed it, though,' he chuckled. 'Their lives would have been dull without me.'

'What about that evening when your things were all moved, and you sat in the armchair out in the front –' began Louisa.

'Ah, that was what you might call the climax,' said the Captain delightedly. 'They told you about that, did they? Well, I thought as I wouldn't be seeing them again, I might as well give them a Grand Finale, so to speak.'

'And a fine spectacle you made of yourself, by all accounts,' said his sister.

'I dare say I did go a bit far,' he admitted, 'but I got carried away. There were they, throwing blue fits all over the place because they were sorry for *me*, and there was I, couldn't see the back of the darned house quick enough! It was dead funny, as they say on the telly – Ah, I listen to the telly, I'm not a back number yet, you know.'

'We did think you might be, but you're certainly not,' said Louisa. She was too much astonished to be anything but candid.

'You mean that sitting in the chair and shouting, that was all *acting*?' said Japhet. His eyes were round with admiration.

'Ah, if I hadn't gone to sea, I reckon I could have taken up the stage,' said the Captain. 'Though I tell you, laugh! I was near splitting myself! Don't know how I kept it up, I don't really. And I was praying they'd clear off before the van came; that would've spoilt it all.'

'The van?'

'For the furniture,' said the Captain's sister. 'Except some bits he decided to leave behind.'

'Where *did* you go, then, that night?' asked Louisa.

'Straight here, of course.' He sounded surprised.

'And you've been here ever since?'

'Ever since.'

'He likes to be near the sea,' his sister told them.

'And were you really, honestly, glad to leave our – your – house?' Louisa asked.

'That gimcrack old place? I reckon if I'd have stopped there I wouldn't be here now,' said the Captain, 'if you see what I mean. Why, I was nearly knocking myself out on the beams every day! It's all right for you townsfolk, I dare say; all very quaint. But when you're born in it you don't see that. I'd rather have a place shipshape than all your wormeaten nooks and crannies.'

'It's historical,' said Japhet, 'or might be.'

'So might I,' laughed the Captain, 'one day!'

'He makes up his own history,' said his sister, sounding dry but amused. 'You never knew such an old story-teller! And the way he can put it on!'

'Did you know there was a well in the garden?' asked Japhet.

'With a dog in it,' said Rose, 'and that boot.'

The Captain looked attentive. 'A dog?' he said.

'We thought it might be,' said Japhet. 'We supposed it was yours.'

'Ah, poor Humbert!' said the Captain, shaking his head. His sister glanced at him sharply. 'But he wasn't a dog, you know,' he went on, 'he was a very special kind of miniature wolf. I brought him home from Alaska, almost an extinct breed; he was an orphan –'

'Noel!' said his sister. Japhet was all agog.

'Might have been here now if I hadn't given him that tot of rum before his dinner. He was drunk, you see, that's how he tripped and fell –'

'*Noel*! Now don't start again! – It's just fairy-stories,' she told the children. 'You mustn't believe a word he says. He's awful, simply awful!' But she looked very fondly at him.

'We like stories,' said Japhet.

'What about the boot?' asked Rose.

'Ah, the boot; I'll tell you that another time. That really *is* a story. There will be another time, won't there?' He looked suddenly gentler. 'It's not often I get young people to see me,' he said, 'and I do appreciate what you've done, by way of routing me out. I do indeed. I only wish Uncle Horatio had kept his engines greased, and we might have all had a good old bust, braced the mainsail and all. As it is; all I can offer is another bulls-eye.'

'How *did* you manage to get here?' said his sister as she handed them round.

'Well,' said Louisa, 'it's my birthday.'

'Really? Many happy returns!'

'Thank you – And you see, they always ask me – my parents, I mean – what I want – so this time, I said to come here.'

'She just said that,' said Japhet, 'and nothing else.'

'They were going to give her a camera,' said Rose, 'or a new tennis racket, but she kept saying she'd rather Bognor.'

'So we all came,' said Japhet.

'It's my present,' Louisa explained. 'A day at the sea – because I wanted to find you, more than anything,' she added simply.

'Well!' The Captain's sister looked, for a moment, almost as if there were a tear in her eye. But of course there couldn't be; she was a grown-up.

'Do you hear that, Noel? You're actually a birthday present!'

'You too,' said Louisa politely; but she did mean it.

'I've never been that before,' said the Captain. 'It's a compliment. Thank you, my dear. Thank you all.'

'It was just lucky I *had* a birthday,' said Louisa. 'Otherwise, I'm not sure how we should have managed.'

'But she would of,' said Rose, 'somehow. Louisa always does.'

'But where are your parents, what have you done with them?' asked the sister.

'We left them on the beach,' Japhet explained. 'They'll be all right.'

'We told them we had a call to pay.'

'Didn't they want to know who, or why?'

'Yes, but we said they'd know all in good time,' Louisa smiled. 'That's what they always tell us. Still, I think perhaps we'd better get back. Mother's apt to stay in the sea too long, and father does get so sunburnt.'

'But you'll come again?' said the Captain. 'We've only just begun to talk yet. I don't get many people to talk to, these days.'

'He just wants an audience for his tall stories, that's what he wants!' said his sister, laughing. 'You should be grateful they've come all this way at all, Noel; but we don't have birthdays every day, you know.'

'We do have them, though,' said Louisa.

'But we can hardly expect to be birthday presents *again*. I should think that's a thing for once in a lifetime. And we are grateful; we do thank you for making us your present.' And she gave Louisa a quick, pecking kiss. Then they all shook hands with the Captain, who followed them out into the hall.

'Actually,' said Japhet, 'I hope we do come again. I like stories. It doesn't matter if they're tall.'

'So do I,' said Rose. 'And bulls-eyes.'

'May we?' said Louisa. 'Really?'

'Of course, but –'

'Then we will,' she announced firmly. And the Captain and his sister felt the same as Rose and Japhet – that if Louisa said they would, they would.

'There was one other thing the Gillingses told us,' she said gaily as they went out of the front door, '– which just goes to show, I mean about getting hold of the wrong end of the stick. They said the Captain was blind!'

There was a slight pause.

'He is,' said the sister quietly.

'. . . And I bet our tramp wasn't at all!' Louisa remarked as they walked down the road, talking about this. 'I bet he was only pretending: I believe he knew what was what all the time. I believe he was a fraud! Anyway, he jolly well managed to clear out with all those things, and without our seeing him, and that means he must have gone some other way, not down the path past the kitchen window.'

'Oh well,' said Japhet, 'I suppose we shall never know.'

And they never did: but it didn't seem to matter much, now that they had found the real Captain.

'You'd *never* think he was blind, would you?' Japhet went on. 'And I don't think he wants you to. He actually makes model boats!'

'Blind people get very clever with their hands,' Louisa said.

'But he twinkled,' said Rose. 'I didn't know they could twinkle.'

'I can't imagine him *not*,' Louisa reflected. 'He's that kind of person.'

'Have we got time to buy an ice cream?' asked Japhet. 'It's your birthday, so I'll pay.'

'They seemed to like those bulls-eyes,' the Captain was saying to his sister. 'Better see we keep some in.' She promised that she always would.

And now, you must imagine the rest. How they did go to see the Captain again, and how he told them taller and taller stories, and how there was always a tin of bulls-eyes on the mantelpiece, because the Captain was convinced that they liked these better than anything else. As a matter of fact, they wouldn't at all have minded a change, but they never said so; even Japhet was a polite boy at heart.

Of course, they still went to see the Gillingses too; but Louisa, at any rate, felt slightly different towards them – almost protective, as if they were the children and she was the grown-up. When they told her bits of local gossip, she would smile to herself and wonder if anybody had been leading them up the garden path again.

'Don't you sometimes feel,' she once said to Georgia, 'very, very *old*?'

'No,' said Georgia; they were lolling on the grass after school dinner. 'You must have eaten too much of that ghastly stodge.'

But Louisa knew it wasn't that. Looking back to the day when she had first decided to find the Captain, she felt she had learned quite a lot since then. There were things she wouldn't do again, things she would, others she might do differently. . . . Anyway, it had been an interesting summer, with its ups and downs.

And it wasn't over yet.

'Really!' said their mother one day towards the end of August, 'that's the seventh tramp we've had here since the holidays began! I can't understand it! I've never made so much tea in all my life!'

Louisa and Japhet and Rose kept quiet. The succession of tramps at the door was something they would rather not discuss. But when they were alone together, Japhet said he thought their father must have been right. There *must* be a secret sign.

'And our tramp must have made a simply enormous one,' Louisa said, 'I wonder if he put a warning about baths.'

'Whatever he put,' said Japhet, 'must have made this house look like a kind of tramps' heaven.'

'Well, it is a nice house,' said Rose.

'Perhaps the sign will somehow get washed away or worn off in the winter,' Louisa said. 'I hope so,' she added, as she saw, from the window, yet another shambling figure hesitate, look at the name on the board in front, and come slowly up the path.

'I'll make it,' she said to her mother, getting down the teapot.

But her mother said wait a minute, she didn't believe this *was* a tramp. She went out to see.

'It isn't!' she reported triumphantly. 'Believe it or not, it's the man who's come to mend the ceiling – at last!'

Japhet and Rose came crowding round, interested and excited. They wanted to see the man's tools, and where he would start, and how he did it. Any new episode was welcome, at the end of the summer holidays. Japhet soon discovered that the man's name was Sam; Rose found that he had a baby at home, and six budgerigars, and that he kept a special thing in his pocket for rolling cigarettes. They settled down to chat with him as he began chipping off the last bits of the old plaster. Who knows, thought Japhet, looking hopefully up through the laths, this might mean a new adventure?

And downstairs, Louisa put a bun on a tray, with yet another cup of tea, and thought of all the things that had happened, the friends they had made, the people they had met, since the day the ceiling fell down.

OTHER TITLES IN THE
BODLEY BOOKSHELF SERIES